BEHIND A MASK,
OR
A WOMAN'S POWER

LECTOR HOUSE PUBLIC DOMAIN WORKS

BEHIND A MASK,
OR A WOMAN'S POWER

LOUISA MAY ALCOTT (A. M. BARNARD)

ISBN: 978-93-5342-339-1

First Published: -

LECTOR HOUSE LLP
E-MAIL: lectorpublishing@gmail.com

BEHIND A MASK
OR
A WOMAN'S POWER

BY

A.M. BARNARD

CONTENTS

CHAPTER I

JEAN MUIR

"Has she come?"

"No, Mamma, not yet."

"I wish it were well over. The thought of it worries and excites me. A cushion for my back, Bella."

And poor, peevish Mrs. Coventry sank into an easy chair with a nervous sigh and the air of a martyr, while her pretty daughter hovered about her with affectionate solicitude.

"Who are they talking of, Lucia?" asked the languid young man lounging on a couch near his cousin, who bent over her tapestry work with a happy smile on her usually haughty face.

"The new governess, Miss Muir. Shall I tell you about her?"

"No, thank you. I have an inveterate aversion to the whole tribe. I've often thanked heaven that I had but one sister, and she a spoiled child, so that I have escaped the infliction of a governess so long."

"How will you bear it now?" asked Lucia.

"Leave the house while she is in it."

"No, you won't. You're too lazy, Gerald," called out a younger and more energetic man, from the recess where he stood teasing his dogs.

"I'll give her a three days' trial; if she proves endurable I shall not disturb myself; if, as I am sure, she is a bore, I'm off anywhere, anywhere out of her way."

"I beg you won't talk in that depressing manner, boys. I dread the coming of a stranger more than you possibly can, but Bella *must* not be neglected; so I have nerved myself to endure this woman, and Lucia is good enough to say she will attend to her after tonight."

"Don't be troubled, Mamma. She is a nice person, I dare say, and when once we are used to her, I've no doubt we shall be glad to have her, it's so dull here just now. Lady Sydney said she was a quiet, accomplished, amiable girl, who needed a home, and would be a help to poor stupid me, so try to like her for my sake."

"I will, dear, but isn't it getting late? I do hope nothing has happened. Did you tell them to send a carriage to the station for her, Gerald?"

"I forgot it. But it's not far, it won't hurt her to walk" was the languid reply.

"It was indolence, not forgetfulness, I know. I'm very sorry; she will think it so rude to leave her to find her way so late. Do go and see to it, Ned."

"Too late, Bella, the train was in some time ago. Give your orders to me next time. Mother and I'll see that they are obeyed," said Edward.

"Ned is just at an age to make a fool of himself for any girl who comes in his way. Have a care of the governess, Lucia, or she will bewitch him."

Gerald spoke in a satirical whisper, but his brother heard him and answered with a good-humored laugh.

"I wish there was any hope of your making a fool of yourself in that way, old fellow. Set me a good example, and I promise to follow it. As for the governess, she is a woman, and should be treated with common civility. I should say a little extra kindness wouldn't be amiss, either, because she is poor, and a stranger."

"That is my dear, good-hearted Ned! We'll stand by poor little Muir, won't we?" And running to her brother, Bella stood on tiptoe to offer him a kiss which he could not refuse, for the rosy lips were pursed up invitingly, and the bright eyes full of sisterly affection.

"I do hope she has come, for, when I make an effort to see anyone, I hate to make it in vain. Punctuality is *such* a virtue, and I know this woman hasn't got it, for she promised to be here at seven, and now it is long after," began Mrs. Coventry, in an injured tone.

Before she could get breath for another complaint, the clock struck seven and the doorbell rang.

"There she is!" cried Bella, and turned toward the door as if to go and meet the newcomer.

But Lucia arrested her, saying authoritatively, "Stay here, child. It is her place to come to you, not yours to go to her."

"Miss Muir," announced a servant, and a little black-robed figure stood in the doorway. For an instant no one stirred, and the governess had time to see and be seen before a word was uttered. All looked at her, and she cast on the household group a keen glance that impressed them curiously; then her eyes fell, and bowing slightly she walked in. Edward came forward and received her with the frank cordiality which nothing could daunt or chill.

"Mother, this is the lady whom you expected. Miss Muir, allow me to apologize for our apparent neglect in not sending for you. There was a mistake about the carriage, or, rather, the lazy fellow to whom the order was given forgot it. Bella, come here."

"Thank you, no apology is needed. I did not expect to be sent for." And the governess meekly sat down without lifting her eyes.

"I am glad to see you. Let me take your things," said Bella, rather shyly, for Gerald, still lounging, watched the fireside group with languid interest, and Lucia never stirred. Mrs. Coventry took a second survey and began:

"You were punctual, Miss Muir, which pleases me. I'm a sad invalid, as Lady Sydney told you, I hope; so that Miss Coventry's lessons will be directed by my niece, and you will go to her for directions, as she knows what I wish. You will excuse me if I ask you a few questions, for Lady Sydney's note was very brief, and I left everything to her judgment."

"Ask anything you like, madam," answered the soft, sad voice.

"You are Scotch, I believe."

"Yes, madam."

"Are your parents living?"

"I have not a relation in the world."

"Dear me, how sad! Do you mind telling me your age?"

"Nineteen." And a smile passed over Miss Muir's lips, as she folded her hands with an air of resignation, for the catechism was evidently to be a long one.

"So young! Lady Sydney mentioned five-and-twenty, I think, didn't she, Bella?"

"No, Mamma, she only said she thought so. Don't ask such questions. It's not pleasant before us all," whispered Bella.

A quick, grateful glance shone on her from the suddenly lifted eyes of Miss Muir, as she said quietly, "I wish I was thirty, but, as I am not, I do my best to look and seem old."

Of course, every one looked at her then, and all felt a touch of pity at the sight of the pale-faced girl in her plain black dress, with no ornament but a little silver cross at her throat. Small, thin, and colorless she was, with yellow hair, gray eyes, and sharply cut, irregular, but very expressive features. Poverty seemed to have set its bond stamp upon her, and life to have had for her more frost than sunshine. But something in the lines of the mouth betrayed strength, and the clear, low voice had a curious mixture of command and entreaty in its varying tones. Not an attractive woman, yet not an ordinary one; and, as she sat there with her delicate hands lying in her lap, her head bent, and a bitter look on her thin face, she was more interesting than many a blithe and blooming girl. Bella's heart warmed to her at once, and she drew her seat nearer, while Edward went back to his dogs that his presence might not embarrass her.

"You have been ill, I think," continued Mrs. Coventry, who considered this fact the most interesting of all she had heard concerning the governess.

"Yes, madam, I left the hospital only a week ago."

"Are you quite sure it is safe to begin teaching so soon?"

"I have no time to lose, and shall soon gain strength here in the country, if you care to keep me."

"And you are fitted to teach music, French, and drawing?"

"I shall endeavor to prove that I am."

"Be kind enough to go and play an air or two. I can judge by your touch; I used to play finely when a girl."

Miss Muir rose, looked about her for the instrument, and seeing it at the other end of the room went toward it, passing Gerald and Lucia as if she did not see them. Bella followed, and in a moment forgot everything in admiration. Miss Muir played like one who loved music and was perfect mistress of her art. She charmed them all by the magic of this spell; even indolent Gerald sat up to listen, and Lucia put down her needle, while Ned watched the slender white fingers as they flew, and wondered at the strength and skill which they possessed.

"Please sing," pleaded Bella, as a brilliant overture ended.

With the same meek obedience Miss Muir complied, and began a little Scotch melody, so sweet, so sad, that the girl's eyes filled, and Mrs. Coventry looked for one of her many pocket-handkerchiefs. But suddenly the music ceased, for, with a vain attempt to support herself, the singer slid from her seat and lay before the startled listeners, as white and rigid as if struck with death. Edward caught her up, and, ordering his brother off the couch, laid her there, while Bella chafed her hands, and her mother rang for her maid. Lucia bathed the poor girl's temples, and Gerald, with unwonted energy, brought a glass of wine. Soon Miss Muir's lips trembled, she sighed, then murmured, tenderly, with a pretty Scotch accent, as if wandering in the past, "Bide wi' me, Mither, I'm sae sick an sad here all alone."

"Take a sip of this, and it will do you good, my dear," said Mrs. Coventry, quite touched by the plaintive words.

The strange voice seemed to recall her. She sat up, looked about her, a little wildly, for a moment, then collected herself and said, with a pathetic look and tone, "Pardon me. I have been on my feet all day, and, in my eagerness to keep my appointment, I forgot to eat since morning. I'm better now; shall I finish the song?"

"By no means. Come and have some tea," said Bella, full of pity and remorse.

"Scene first, very well done," whispered Gerald to his cousin.

Miss Muir was just before them, apparently listening to Mrs. Coventry's remarks upon fainting fits; but she heard, and looked over her shoulders with a gesture like Rachel. Her eyes were gray, but at that instant they seemed black with some strong emotion of anger, pride, or defiance. A curious smile passed over her face as she bowed, and said in her penetrating voice, "Thanks. The last scene shall be still better."

Young Coventry was a cool, indolent man, seldom conscious of any emotion, any passion, pleasurable or otherwise; but at the look, the tone of the governess, he experienced a new sensation, indefinable, yet strong. He colored and, for the first time in his life, looked abashed. Lucia saw it, and hated Miss Muir with a sudden hatred; for, in all the years she had passed with her cousin, no look or word of hers had possessed such power. Coventry was himself again in an instant, with no trace of that passing change, but a look of interest in his usually dreamy eyes, and a touch of anger in his sarcastic voice.

"What a melodramatic young lady! I shall go tomorrow."

Lucia laughed, and was well pleased when he sauntered away to bring her a cup of tea from the table where a little scene was just taking place. Mrs. Coventry had sunk into her chair again, exhausted by the flurry of the fainting fit. Bella was busied about her; and Edward, eager to feed the pale governess, was awkwardly trying to make the tea, after a beseeching glance at his cousin which she did not choose to answer. As he upset the caddy and uttered a despairing exclamation, Miss Muir quietly took her place behind the urn, saying with a smile, and a shy glance at the young man, "Allow me to assume my duty at once, and serve you all. I understand the art of making people comfortable in this way. The scoop, please. I can gather this up quite well alone, if you will tell me how your mother likes her tea."

Edward pulled a chair to the table and made merry over his mishaps, while Miss Muir performed her little task with a skill and grace that made it pleasant to watch her. Coventry lingered a moment after she had given him a steaming cup, to observe her more nearly, while he asked a question or two of his brother. She took no more notice of him than if he had been a statue, and in the middle of the one remark he addressed to her, she rose to take the sugar basin to Mrs. Coventry, who was quite won by the modest, domestic graces of the new governess.

"Really, my dear, you are a treasure; I haven't tasted such tea since my poor maid Ellis died. Bella never makes it good, and Miss Lucia always forgets the cream. Whatever you do you seem to do well, and that is *such* a comfort."

"Let me always do this for you, then. It will be a pleasure, madam." And Miss Muir came back to her seat with a faint color in her cheek which improved her much.

"My brother asked if young Sydney was at home when you left," said Edward, for Gerald would not take the trouble to repeat the question.

Miss Muir fixed her eyes on Coventry, and answered with a slight tremor of the lips, "No, he left home some weeks ago."

The young man went back to his cousin, saying, as he threw himself down beside her, "I shall not go tomorrow, but wait till the three days are out."

"Why?" demanded Lucia.

Lowering his voice he said, with a significant nod toward the governess, "Because I have a fancy that she is at the bottom of Sydney's mystery. He's not been himself lately, and now he is gone without a word. I rather like romances in real life, if they are not too long, or difficult to read."

"Do you think her pretty?"

"Far from it, a most uncanny little specimen."

"Then why fancy Sydney loves her?"

"He is an oddity, and likes sensations and things of that sort."

"What do you mean, Gerald?"

"Get the Muir to look at you, as she did at me, and you will understand. Will you have another cup, Juno?"

"Yes, please." She liked to have him wait upon her, for he did it to no other woman except his mother.

Before he could slowly rise, Miss Muir glided to them with another cup on the salver; and, as Lucia took it with a cold nod, the girl said under her breath, "I think it honest to tell you that I possess a quick ear, and cannot help hearing what is said anywhere in the room. What you say of me is of no consequence, but you may speak of things which you prefer I should not hear; therefore, allow me to warn you." And she was gone again as noiselessly as she came.

"How do you like that?" whispered Coventry, as his cousin sat looking after the girl, with a disturbed expression.

"What an uncomfortable creature to have in the house! I am very sorry I urged her coming, for your mother has taken a fancy to her, and it will be hard to get rid of her," said Lucia, half angry, half amused.

"Hush, she hears every word you say. I know it by the expression of her face, for Ned is talking about horses, and she looks as haughty as ever you did, and that is saying much. Faith, this is getting interesting."

"Hark, she is speaking; I want to hear," and Lucia laid her hand on her cousin's lips. He kissed it, and then idly amused himself with turning the rings to and fro on the slender fingers.

"I have been in France several years, madam, but my friend died and I came back to be with Lady Sydney, till—" Muir paused an instant, then added, slowly, "till I fell ill. It was a contagious fever, so I went of my own accord to the hospital, not wishing to endanger her."

"Very right, but are you sure there is no danger of infection now?" asked Mrs. Coventry anxiously.

"None, I assure you. I have been well for some time, but did not leave because I preferred to stay there, than to return to Lady Sydney."

"No quarrel, I hope? No trouble of any kind?"

"No quarrel, but—well, why not? You have a right to know, and I will not make a foolish mystery out of a very simple thing. As your family, only, is present, I may tell the truth. I did not go back on the young gentleman's account. Please ask no more."

"Ah, I see. Quite prudent and proper, Miss Muir. I shall never allude to it again. Thank you for your frankness. Bella, you will be careful not to mention this to young friends; girls gossip sadly, and it would annoy Lady Sydney beyond everything to have this talked of."

"Very neighborly of Lady S. to send the dangerous young lady here, where there are *two* young gentlemen to be captivated. I wonder why she didn't keep Sydney after she had caught him," murmured Coventry to his cousin.

"Because she had the utmost contempt for a titled fool." Miss Muir dropped the words almost into his ear, as she bent to take her shawl from the sofa corner.

"How the deuce did she get there?" ejaculated Coventry, looking as if he had received another sensation. "She has spirit, though, and upon my word I pity Sydney, if he did try to dazzle her, for he must have got a splendid dismissal."

"Come and play billiards. You promised, and I hold you to your word," said Lucia, rising with decision, for Gerald was showing too much interest in another to suit Miss Beaufort.

"I am, as ever, your most devoted. My mother is a charming woman, but I find our evening parties slightly dull, when only my own family are present. Good night, Mamma." He shook hands with his mother, whose pride and idol he was, and, with a comprehensive nod to the others, strolled after his cousin.

"Now they are gone we can be quite cozy, and talk over things, for I don't mind Ned any more than I do his dogs," said Bella, settling herself on her mother's footstool.

"I merely wish to say, Miss Muir, that my daughter has never had a governess and is sadly backward for a girl of sixteen. I want you to pass the mornings with her, and get her on as rapidly as possible. In the afternoon you will walk or drive with her, and in the evening sit with us here, if you like, or amuse yourself as you please. While in the country we are very quiet, for I cannot bear much company, and when my sons want gaiety, they go away for it. Miss Beaufort oversees the servants, and takes my place as far as possible. I am very delicate and keep my room till evening, except for an airing at noon. We will try each other for a month, and I hope we shall get on quite comfortably together."

"I shall do my best, madam."

One would not have believed that the meek, spiritless voice which uttered these words was the same that had startled Coventry a few minutes before, nor that the pale, patient face could ever have kindled with such sudden fire as that which looked over Miss Muir's shoulder when she answered her young host's speech.

Edward thought within himself, Poor little woman! She has had a hard life.

We will try and make it easier while she is here; and began his charitable work by suggesting that she might be tired. She acknowledged she was, and Bella led her away to a bright, cozy room, where with a pretty little speech and a good-night kiss she left her.

When alone Miss Muir's conduct was decidedly peculiar. Her first act was to clench her hands and mutter between her teeth, with passionate force, "I'll not fail again if there is power in a woman's wit and will!" She stood a moment motionless, with an expression of almost fierce disdain on her face, then shook her clenched hand as if menacing some unseen enemy. Next she laughed, and shrugged her shoulders with a true French shrug, saying low to herself, "Yes, the last scene *shall* be better than the first. *Mon dieu*, how tired and hungry I am!"

Kneeling before the one small trunk which held her worldly possessions, she opened it, drew out a flask, and mixed a glass of some ardent cordial, which she seemed to enjoy extremely as she sat on the carpet, musing, while her quick eyes examined every corner of the room.

"Not bad! It will be a good field for me to work in, and the harder the task the better I shall like it. *Merci*, old friend. You put heart and courage into me when nothing else will. Come, the curtain is down, so I may be myself for a few hours, if actresses ever are themselves."

Still sitting on the floor she unbound and removed the long abundant braids from her head, wiped the pink from her face, took out several pearly teeth, and slipping off her dress appeared herself indeed, a haggard, worn, and moody woman of thirty at least. The metamorphosis was wonderful, but the disguise was more in the expression she assumed than in any art of costume or false adornment. Now she was alone, and her mobile features settled into their natural expression, weary, hard, bitter. She had been lovely once, happy, innocent, and tender; but nothing of all this remained to the gloomy woman who leaned there brooding over some wrong, or loss, or disappointment which had darkened all her life. For an hour she sat so, sometimes playing absently with the scanty locks that hung about her face, sometimes lifting the glass to her lips as if the fiery draught warmed her cold blood; and once she half uncovered her breast to eye with a terrible glance the scar of a newly healed wound. At last she rose and crept to bed, like one worn out with weariness and mental pain.

CHAPTER II
A GOOD BEGINNING

Only the housemaids were astir when Miss Muir left her room next morning and quietly found her way into the garden. As she walked, apparently intent upon the flowers, her quick eye scrutinized the fine old house and its picturesque surroundings.

"Not bad," she said to herself, adding, as she passed into the adjoining park, "but the other may be better, and I will have the best."

Walking rapidly, she came out at length upon the wide green lawn which lay before the ancient hall where Sir John Coventry lived in solitary splendor. A stately old place, rich in oaks, well-kept shrubberies, gay gardens, sunny terraces, carved gables, spacious rooms, liveried servants, and every luxury befitting the ancestral home of a rich and honorable race. Miss Muir's eyes brightened as she looked, her step grew firmer, her carriage prouder, and a smile broke over her face; the smile of one well pleased at the prospect of the success of some cherished hope. Suddenly her whole air changed, she pushed back her hat, clasped her hands loosely before her, and seemed absorbed in girlish admiration of the fair scene that could not fail to charm any beauty-loving eye. The cause of this rapid change soon appeared. A hale, handsome man, between fifty and sixty, came through the little gate leading to the park, and, seeing the young stranger, paused to examine her. He had only time for a glance, however; she seemed conscious of his presence in a moment, turned with a startled look, uttered an exclamation of surprise, and looked as if hesitating whether to speak or run away. Gallant Sir John took off his hat and said, with the old-fashioned courtesy which became him well, "I beg your pardon for disturbing you, young lady. Allow me to atone for it by inviting you to walk where you will, and gather what flowers you like. I see you love them, so pray make free with those about you."

With a charming air of maidenly timidity and artlessness, Miss Muir replied, "Oh, thank you, sir! But it is I who should ask pardon for trespassing. I never should have dared if I had not known that Sir John was absent. I always wanted to see this fine old place, and ran over the first thing, to satisfy myself."

"And *are* you satisfied?" he asked, with a smile.

"More than satisfied—I'm charmed; for it is the most beautiful spot I ever saw, and I've seen many famous seats, both at home and abroad," she answered enthusiastically.

"The Hall is much flattered, and so would its master be if he heard you," began the gentleman, with an odd expression.

"I should not praise it to him—at least, not as freely as I have to you, sir," said the girl, with eyes still turned away.

"Why not?" asked her companion, looking much amused.

"I should be afraid. Not that I dread Sir John; but I've heard so many beautiful and noble things about him, and respect him so highly, that I should not dare to say much, lest he should see how I admire and—"

"And what, young lady? Finish, if you please."

"I was going to say, love him. I will say it, for he is an old man, and one cannot help loving virtue and bravery."

Miss Muir looked very earnest and pretty as she spoke, standing there with the sunshine glinting on her yellow hair, delicate face, and downcast eyes. Sir John was not a vain man, but he found it pleasant to hear himself commended by this unknown girl, and felt redoubled curiosity to learn who she was. Too well-bred to ask, or to abash her by avowing what she seemed unconscious of, he left both discoveries to chance; and when she turned, as if to retrace her steps, he offered her the handful of hothouse flowers which he held, saying, with a gallant bow, "In Sir John's name let me give you my little nosegay, with thanks for your good opinion, which, I assure you, is not entirely deserved, for I know him well."

Miss Muir looked up quickly, eyed him an instant, then dropped her eyes, and, coloring deeply, stammered out, "I did not know—I beg your pardon—you are too kind, Sir John."

He laughed like a boy, asking, mischievously, "Why call me Sir John? How do you know that I am not the gardener or the butler?"

"I did not see your face before, and no one but yourself would say that any praise was undeserved," murmured Miss Muir, still overcome with girlish confusion.

"Well, well, we will let that pass, and the next time you come we will be properly introduced. Bella always brings her friends to the Hall, for I am fond of young people."

"I am not a friend. I am only Miss Coventry's governess." And Miss Muir dropped a meek curtsy. A slight change passed over Sir John's manner. Few would have perceived it, but Miss Muir felt it at once, and bit her lips with an angry feeling at her heart. With a curious air of pride, mingled with respect, she accepted the still offered bouquet, returned Sir John's parting bow, and tripped away, leaving the old gentleman to wonder where Mrs. Coventry found such a piquant little governess.

"That is done, and very well for a beginning," she said to herself as she approached the house.

In a green paddock close by fed a fine horse, who lifted up his head and eyed her inquiringly, like one who expected a greeting. Following a sudden impulse, she entered the paddock and, pulling a handful of clover, invited the creature to come and eat. This was evidently a new proceeding on the part of a lady, and the horse careered about as if bent on frightening the newcomer away.

"I see," she said aloud, laughing to herself. "I am not your master, and you rebel. Nevertheless, I'll conquer you, my fine brute."

Seating herself in the grass, she began to pull daisies, singing idly the while, as if unconscious of the spirited prancings of the horse. Presently he drew nearer, sniffing curiously and eyeing her with surprise. She took no notice, but plaited the daisies and sang on as if he was not there. This seemed to pique the petted creature, for, slowly approaching, he came at length so close that he could smell her little foot and nibble at her dress. Then she offered the clover, uttering caressing words and making soothing sounds, till by degrees and with much coquetting, the horse permitted her to stroke his glossy neck and smooth his mane.

It was a pretty sight—the slender figure in the grass, the high-spirited horse bending his proud head to her hand. Edward Coventry, who had watched the scene, found it impossible to restrain himself any longer and, leaping the wall, came to join the group, saying, with mingled admiration and wonder in countenance and voice, "Good morning, Miss Muir. If I had not seen your skill and courage proved before my eyes, I should be alarmed for your safety. Hector is a wild, wayward beast, and has damaged more than one groom who tried to conquer him."

"Good morning, Mr. Coventry. Don't tell tales of this noble creature, who has not deceived my faith in him. Your grooms did not know how to win his heart, and so subdue his spirit without breaking it."

Miss Muir rose as she spoke, and stood with her hand on Hector's neck while he ate the grass which she had gathered in the skirt of her dress.

"You have the secret, and Hector is your subject now, though heretofore he has rejected all friends but his master. Will you give him his morning feast? I always bring him bread and play with him before breakfast."

"Then you are not jealous?" And she looked up at him with eyes so bright and beautiful in expression that the young man wondered he had not observed them before.

"Not I. Pet him as much as you will; it will do him good. He is a solitary fellow, for he scorns his own kind and lives alone, like his master," he added, half to himself.

"Alone, with such a happy home, Mr. Coventry?" And a softly compassionate glance stole from the bright eyes.

"That was an ungrateful speech, and I retract it for Bella's sake. Younger sons have no position but such as they can make for themselves, you know, and I've had no chance yet."

"Younger sons! I thought—I beg pardon." And Miss Muir paused, as if remembering that she had no right to question.

Edward smiled and answered frankly, "Nay, don't mind me. You thought I was the heir, perhaps. Whom did you take my brother for last night?"

"For some guest who admired Miss Beaufort. I did not hear his name, nor observe him enough to discover who he was. I saw only your kind mother, your charming little sister, and—"

She stopped there, with a half-shy, half-grateful look at the young man which finished the sentence better than any words. He was still a boy, in spite of his one-and-twenty years, and a little color came into his brown cheek as the eloquent eyes met his and fell before them.

"Yes, Bella is a capital girl, and one can't help loving her. I know you'll get her on, for, really, she is the most delightful little dunce. My mother's ill health and Bella's devotion to her have prevented our attending to her education before. Next winter, when we go to town, she is to come out, and must be prepared for that great event, you know," he said, choosing a safe subject.

"I shall do my best. And that reminds me that I should report myself to her, instead of enjoying myself here. When one has been ill and shut up a long time, the country is so lovely one is apt to forget duty for pleasure. Please remind me if I am negligent, Mr. Coventry."

"That name belongs to Gerald. I'm only Mr. Ned here," he said as they walked toward the house, while Hector followed to the wall and sent a sonorous farewell after them.

Bella came running to meet them, and greeted Miss Muir as if she had made up her mind to like her heartily. "What a lovely bouquet you have got! I never can arrange flowers prettily, which vexes me, for Mamma is so fond of them and cannot go out herself. You have charming taste," she said, examining the graceful posy which Miss Muir had much improved by adding feathery grasses, delicate ferns, and fragrant wild flowers to Sir John's exotics.

Putting them into Bella's hand, she said, in a winning way, "Take them to your mother, then, and ask her if I may have the pleasure of making her a daily nosegay; for I should find real delight in doing it, if it would please her."

"How kind you are! Of course it would please her. I'll take them to her while the dew is still on them." And away flew Bella, eager to give both the flowers and the pretty message to the poor invalid.

Edward stopped to speak to the gardener, and Miss Muir went up the steps alone. The long hall was lined with portraits, and pacing slowly down it she examined them with interest. One caught her eye, and, pausing before it, she scrutinized it carefully. A young, beautiful, but very haughty female face. Miss Muir suspected at once who it was, and gave a decided nod, as if she saw and caught at some unexpected chance. A soft rustle behind her made her look around, and, seeing Lucia, she bowed, half turned, as if for another glance at the picture, and said, as if involuntarily, "How beautiful it is! May I ask if it is an ancestor, Miss Beaufort?"

"It is the likeness of my mother" was the reply, given with a softened voice and eyes that looked up tenderly.

"Ah, I might have known, from the resemblance, but I scarcely saw you last night. Excuse my freedom, but Lady Sydney treated me as a friend, and I forget my position. Allow me."

As she spoke, Miss Muir stooped to return the handkerchief which had fallen from Lucia's hand, and did so with a humble mien which touched the other's heart; for, though a proud, it was also a very generous one.

"Thank you. Are you better, this morning?" she said, graciously. And having received an affirmative reply, she added, as she walked on, "I will show you to the breakfast room, as Bella is not here. It is a very informal meal with us, for my aunt is never down and my cousins are very irregular in their hours. You can always have yours when you like, without waiting for us if you are an early riser."

Bella and Edward appeared before the others were seated, and Miss Muir quietly ate her breakfast, feeling well satisfied with her hour's work. Ned recounted her exploit with Hector, Bella delivered her mother's thanks for the flowers, and Lucia more than once recalled, with pardonable vanity, that the governess had compared her to her lovely mother, expressing by a look as much admiration for the living likeness as for the painted one. All kindly did their best to make the pale girl feel at home, and their cordial manner seemed to warm and draw her out; for soon she put off her sad, meek air and entertained them with gay anecdotes of her life in Paris, her travels in Russia when governess in Prince Jermadoff's family, and all manner of witty stories that kept them interested and merry long after the meal was over. In the middle of an absorbing adventure, Coventry came in, nodded lazily, lifted his brows, as if surprised at seeing the governess there, and began his breakfast as if the ennui of another day had already taken possession of him. Miss Muir stopped short, and no entreaties could induce her to go on.

"Another time I will finish it, if you like. Now Miss Bella and I should be at our books." And she left the room, followed by her pupil, taking no notice of the young master of the house, beyond a graceful bow in answer to his careless nod.

"Merciful creature! she goes when I come, and does not make life unendurable by moping about before my eyes. Does she belong to the moral, the melancholy, the romantic, or the dashing class, Ned?" said Gerald, lounging over his coffee as he did over everything he attempted.

"To none of them; she is a capital little woman. I wish you had seen her tame Hector this morning." And Edward repeated his story.

"Not a bad move on her part," said Coventry in reply. "She must be an observing as well as an energetic young person, to discover your chief weakness and attack it so soon. First tame the horse, and then the master. It will be amusing to watch the game, only I shall be under the painful necessity of checkmating you both, if it gets serious."

"You needn't exert yourself, old fellow, on my account. If I was not above thinking ill of an inoffensive girl, I should say you were the prize best worth winning, and advise you to take care of your own heart, if you've got one, which I rather doubt."

"I often doubt it, myself; but I fancy the little Scotchwoman will not be able to satisfy either of us upon that point. How does your highness like her?" asked Coventry of his cousin, who sat near him.

"Better than I thought I should. She is well-bred, unassuming, and very entertaining when she likes. She has told us some of the wittiest stories I've heard for a long time. Didn't our laughter wake you?" replied Lucia.

"Yes. Now atone for it by amusing me with a repetition of these witty tales."

"That is impossible; her accent and manner are half the charm," said Ned. "I wish you had kept away ten minutes longer, for your appearance spoilt the best story of all."

"Why didn't she go on?" asked Coventry, with a ray of curiosity.

"You forget that she overheard us last night, and must feel that you consider her a bore. She has pride, and no woman forgets speeches like those you made," answered Lucia.

"Or forgives them, either, I believe. Well, I must be resigned to languish under her displeasure then. On Sydney's account I take a slight interest in her; not that I expect to learn anything from her, for a woman with a mouth like that never confides or confesses anything. But I have a fancy to see what captivated him; for captivated he was, beyond a doubt, and by no lady whom he met in society. Did you ever hear anything of it, Ned?" asked Gerald.

"I'm not fond of scandal or gossip, and never listen to either." With which remark Edward left the room.

Lucia was called out by the housekeeper a moment after, and Coventry left to the society most wearisome to him, namely his own. As he entered, he had caught a part of the story which Miss Muir had been telling, and it had excited his curiosity so much that he found himself wondering what the end could be and wishing that he might hear it.

What the deuce did she run away for, when I came in? he thought. If she *is* amusing, she must make herself useful; for it's intensely dull, I own, here, in spite of Lucia. Hey, what's that?

It was a rich, sweet voice, singing a brilliant Italian air, and singing it with an expression that made the music doubly delicious. Stepping out of the French window, Coventry strolled along the sunny terrace, enjoying the song with the relish of a connoisseur. Others followed, and still he walked and listened, forgetful of weariness or tune. As one exquisite air ended, he involuntarily applauded. Miss Muir's face appeared for an instant, then vanished, and no more music followed, though Coventry lingered, hoping to hear the voice again. For music was the one thing of which he never wearied, and neither Lucia nor Bella possessed skill enough to charm him. For an hour he loitered on the terrace or the lawn, basking in the sunshine, too indolent to seek occupation or society. At length Bella came out, hat in hand, and nearly stumbled over her brother, who lay on the grass.

"You lazy man, have you been dawdling here all this time?" she said, looking down at him.

"No, I've been very busy. Come and tell me how you've got on with the little dragon."

"Can't stop. She bade me take a run after my French, so that I might be ready for my drawing, and so I must."

"It's too warm to run. Sit down and amuse your deserted brother, who has had no society but bees and lizards for an hour."

He drew her down as he spoke, and Bella obeyed; for, in spite of his indolence, he was one to whom all submitted without dreaming of refusal.

"What have you been doing? Muddling your poor little brains with all manner of elegant rubbish?"

"No, I've been enjoying myself immensely. Jean is *so* interesting, so kind and clever. She didn't bore me with stupid grammar, but just talked to me in such pretty French that I got on capitally, and like it as I never expected to, after Lucia's dull way of teaching it."

"What did you talk about?"

"Oh, all manner of things. She asked questions, and I answered, and she corrected me."

"Questions about our affairs, I suppose?"

"Not one. She don't care two sous for us or our affairs. I thought she might like to know what sort of people we were, so I told her about Papa's sudden death, Uncle John, and you, and Ned; but in the midst of it she said, in her quiet way, 'You are getting too confidential, my dear. It is not best to talk too freely of one's affairs to strangers. Let us speak of something else.'"

"What were you talking of when she said that, Bell?"

"You."

"Ah, then no wonder she was bored."

"She was tired of my chatter, and didn't hear half I said; for she was busy sketching something for me to copy, and thinking of something more interesting than the Coventrys."

"How do you know?"

"By the expression of her face. Did you like her music, Gerald?"

"Yes. Was she angry when I clapped?"

"She looked surprised, then rather proud, and shut the piano at once, though I begged her to go on. Isn't Jean a pretty name?"

"Not bad; but why don't you call her Miss Muir?"

"She begged me not. She hates it, and loves to be called Jean, alone. I've imagined such a nice little romance about her, and someday I shall tell her, for I'm sure she has had a love trouble."

"Don't get such nonsense into your head, but follow Miss Muir's well-bred example and don't be curious about other people's affairs. Ask her to sing tonight; it amuses me."

"She won't come down, I think. We've planned to read and work in my boudoir, which is to be our study now. Mamma will stay in her room, so you and Lucia can have the drawing room all to yourselves."

"Thank you. What will Ned do?"

"He will amuse Mamma, he says. Dear old Ned! I wish you'd stir about and get him his commission. He is so impatient to be doing something and yet so proud he won't ask again, after you have neglected it so many times and refused Uncle's help."

"I'll attend to it very soon; don't worry me, child. He will do very well for a time, quietly here with us."

"You always say that, yet you know he chafes and is unhappy at being dependent on you. Mamma and I don't mind; but he is a man, and it frets him. He said he'd take matters into his own hands soon, and then you may be sorry you were so slow in helping him."

"Miss Muir is looking out of the window. You'd better go and take your run, else she will scold."

"Not she. I'm not a bit afraid of her, she's so gentle and sweet. I'm fond of her already. You'll get as brown as Ned, lying here in the sun. By the way, Miss Muir agrees with me in thinking him handsomer than you."

"I admire her taste and quite agree with her."

"She said he was manly, and that was more attractive than beauty in a man. She does express things so nicely. Now I'm off." And away danced Bella, humming the burden of Miss Muir's sweetest song.

"'Energy is more attractive than beauty in a man.' She is right, but how the deuce *can* a man be energetic, with nothing to expend his energies upon?" mused Coventry, with his hat over his eyes.

A few moments later, the sweep of a dress caught his ear. Without stirring, a sidelong glance showed him Miss Muir coming across the terrace, as if to join Bella. Two stone steps led down to the lawn. He lay near them, and Miss Muir did not see him till close upon him. She started and slipped on the last step, recovered herself, and glided on, with a glance of unmistakable contempt as she passed the recumbent figure of the apparent sleeper. Several things in Bella's report had nettled him, but this look made him angry, though he would not own it, even to himself.

"Gerald, come here, quick!" presently called Bella, from the rustic seat where she stood beside her governess, who sat with her hand over her face as if in pain.

Gathering himself up, Coventry slowly obeyed, but involuntarily quickened his pace as he heard Miss Muir say, "Don't call him; *he* can do nothing"; for the emphasis on the word "he" was very significant.

"What is it, Bella?" he asked, looking rather wider awake than usual.

"You startled Miss Muir and made her turn her ankle. Now help her to the house, for she is in great pain; and don't lie there anymore to frighten people like a snake in the grass," said his sister petulantly.

"I beg your pardon. Will you allow me?" And Coventry offered his arm.

Miss Muir looked up with the expression which annoyed him and answered coldly, "Thank you, Miss Bella will do as well."

"Permit me to doubt that." And with a gesture too decided to be resisted, Coventry drew her arm through his and led her into the house. She submitted quietly, said the pain would soon be over, and when settled on the couch in Bella's room dismissed him with the briefest thanks. Considering the unwonted exertion he had made, he thought she might have been a little more grateful, and went away to Lucia, who always brightened when he came.

No more was seen of Miss Muir till teatime; for now, while the family were in retirement, they dined early and saw no company. The governess had excused herself at dinner, but came down in the evening a little paler than usual and with a slight limp in her gait. Sir John was there, talking with his nephew, and they merely acknowledged her presence by the sort of bow which gentlemen bestow on governesses. As she slowly made her way to her place behind the urn, Coventry said to his brother, "Take her a footstool, and ask her how she is, Ned." Then, as if necessary to account for his politeness to his uncle, he explained how he was the cause of the accident.

"Yes, yes. I understand. Rather a nice little person, I fancy. Not exactly a beauty, but accomplished and well-bred, which is better for one of her class."

"Some tea, Sir John?" said a soft voice at his elbow, and there was Miss Muir, offering cups to the gentlemen.

"Thank you, thank you," said Sir John, sincerely hoping she had overheard him.

As Coventry took his, he said graciously, "You are very forgiving, Miss Muir, to wait upon me, after I have caused you so much pain."

"It is my duty, sir" was her reply, in a tone which plainly said, "but not my pleasure." And she returned to her place, to smile, and chat, and be charming, with Bella and her brother.

Lucia, hovering near her uncle and Gerald, kept them to herself, but was disturbed to find that their eyes often wandered to the cheerful group about the table, and that their attention seemed distracted by the frequent bursts of laughter and fragments of animated conversation which reached them. In the midst of an account of a tragic affair which she endeavored to make as interesting and pathetic as possible, Sir John burst into a hearty laugh, which betrayed that he had been listening to a livelier story than her own. Much annoyed, she said hastily, "I knew it would be so! Bella has no idea of the proper manner in which to treat a governess. She and Ned will forget the difference of rank and spoil that person for her work. She is inclined to be presumptuous already, and if my aunt won't trouble herself to give Miss Muir a hint in time, I shall."

"Wait until she has finished that story, I beg of you," said Coventry, for Sir John was already off.

"If you find that nonsense so entertaining, why don't you follow Uncle's example? I don't need you."

"Thank you. I will." And Lucia was deserted.

But Miss Muir had ended and, beckoning to Bella, left the room, as if quite unconscious of the honor conferred upon her or the dullness she left behind her. Ned went up to his mother, Gerald returned to make his peace with Lucia, and, bidding them good-night, Sir John turned homeward. Strolling along the terrace, he came to the lighted window of Bella's study, and wishing to say a word to her, he half pushed aside the curtain and looked in. A pleasant little scene. Bella working busily, and near her in a low chair, with the light falling on her fair hair and delicate profile, sat Miss Muir reading aloud. "Novels!" thought Sir John, and smiled at them for a pair of romantic girls. But pausing to listen a moment before he spoke, he found it was no novel, but history, read with a fluency which made every fact interesting, every sketch of character memorable, by the dramatic effect given to it. Sir John was fond of history, and failing eyesight often curtailed his favorite amusement. He had tried readers, but none suited him, and he had given up the plan. Now as he listened, he thought how pleasantly the smoothly flowing voice would wile away his evenings, and he envied Bella her new acquisition.

A bell rang, and Bella sprang up, saying, "Wait for me a minute. I must run to Mamma, and then we will go on with this charming prince."

Away she went, and Sir John was about to retire as quietly as he came, when Miss Muir's peculiar behavior arrested him for an instant. Dropping the book, she threw her arms across the table, laid her head down upon them, and broke into a passion of tears, like one who could bear restraint no longer. Shocked and amazed, Sir John stole away; but all that night the kindhearted gentleman puzzled his brains with conjectures about his niece's interesting young governess, quite unconscious that she intended he should do so.

CHAPTER III

PASSION AND PIQUE

For several weeks the most monotonous tranquillity seemed to reign at Coventry House, and yet, unseen, unsuspected, a storm was gathering. The arrival of Miss Muir seemed to produce a change in everyone, though no one could have explained how or why. Nothing could be more unobtrusive and retiring than her manners. She was devoted to Bella, who soon adored her, and was only happy when in her society. She ministered in many ways to Mrs. Coventry's comfort, and that lady declared there never was such a nurse. She amused, interested and won Edward with her wit and womanly sympathy. She made Lucia respect and envy her for her accomplishments, and piqued indolent Gerald by her persistent avoidance of him, while Sir John was charmed with her respectful deference and the graceful little attentions she paid him in a frank and artless way, very winning to the lonely old man. The very servants liked her; and instead of being, what most governesses are, a forlorn creature hovering between superiors and inferiors, Jean Muir was the life of the house, and the friend of all but two.

Lucia disliked her, and Coventry distrusted her; neither could exactly say why, and neither owned the feeling, even to themselves. Both watched her covertly yet found no shortcoming anywhere. Meek, modest, faithful, and invariably sweet-tempered—they could complain of nothing and wondered at their own doubts, though they could not banish them.

It soon came to pass that the family was divided, or rather that two members were left very much to themselves. Pleading timidity, Jean Muir kept much in Bella's study and soon made it such a pleasant little nook that Ned and his mother, and often Sir John, came in to enjoy the music, reading, or cheerful chat which made the evenings so gay. Lucia at first was only too glad to have her cousin to herself, and he too lazy to care what went on about him. But presently he wearied of her society, for she was not a brilliant girl, and possessed few of those winning arts which charm a man and steal into his heart. Rumors of the merry-makings that went on reached him and made him curious to share them; echoes of fine music went sounding through the house, as he lounged about the empty drawing room; and peals of laughter reached him while listening to Lucia's grave discourse.

She soon discovered that her society had lost its charm, and the more eagerly she tried to please him, the more signally she failed. Before long Coventry fell into a habit of strolling out upon the terrace of an evening, and amusing himself by passing and repassing the window of Bella's room, catching glimpses of what was going on and reporting the result of his observations to Lucia, who was too proud to ask admission to the happy circle or to seem to desire it.

"I shall go to London tomorrow, Lucia," Gerald said one evening, as he came back from what he called "a survey," looking very much annoyed.

"To London?" exclaimed his cousin, surprised.

"Yes, I must bestir myself and get Ned his commission, or it will be all over with him."

"How do you mean?"

"He is falling in love as fast as it is possible for a boy to do it. That girl has bewitched him, and he will make a fool of himself very soon, unless I put a stop to it."

"I was afraid she would attempt a flirtation. These persons always do, they are such a mischief-making race."

"Ah, but there you are wrong, as far as little Muir is concerned. She does not flirt, and Ned has too much sense and spirit to be caught by a silly coquette. She treats him like an elder sister, and mingles the most attractive friendliness with a quiet dignity that captivates the boy. I've been watching them, and there he is, devouring her with his eyes, while she reads a fascinating novel in the most fascinating style. Bella and Mamma are absorbed in the tale, and see nothing; but Ned makes himself the hero, Miss Muir the heroine, and lives the love scene with all the ardor of a man whose heart has just waked up. Poor lad! Poor lad!"

Lucia looked at her cousin, amazed by the energy with which he spoke, the anxiety in his usually listless face. The change became him, for it showed what he might be, making one regret still more what he was. Before she could speak, he was gone again, to return presently, laughing, yet looking a little angry.

"What now?" she asked.

"'Listeners never hear any good of themselves' is the truest of proverbs. I stopped a moment to look at Ned, and heard the following flattering remarks. Mamma is gone, and Ned was asking little Muir to sing that delicious barcarole she gave us the other evening.

"'Not now, not here,' she said.

"'Why not? You sang it in the drawing room readily enough,' said Ned, imploringly.

"'That is a very different thing,' and she looked at him with a little shake of the head, for he was folding his hands and doing the passionate pathetic.

"'Come and sing it there then,' said innocent Bella. 'Gerald likes your voice so much, and complains that you will never sing to him.'

"'He never asks me,' said Muir, with an odd smile.

"'He is too lazy, but he wants to hear you.'

"'When he asks me, I will sing—if I feel like it.' And she shrugged her shoulders with a provoking gesture of indifference.

"'But it amuses him, and he gets so bored down here,' began stupid little Bella. 'Don't be shy or proud, Jean, but come and entertain the poor old fellow.'

"'No, thank you. I engaged to teach Miss Coventry, not to amuse Mr. Coventry' was all the answer she got.

"'You amuse Ned, why not Gerald? Are you afraid of him?' asked Bella.

"Miss Muir laughed, such a scornful laugh, and said, in that peculiar tone of hers, 'I cannot fancy anyone being *afraid* of your elder brother.'

"'I am, very often, and so would you be, if you ever saw him angry,' And Bella looked as if I'd beaten her.

"'Does he ever wake up enough to be angry?' asked that girl, with an air of surprise. Here Ned broke into a fit of laughter, and they are at it now, I fancy, by the sound."

"Their foolish gossip is not worth getting excited about, but I certainly would send Ned away. It's no use trying to get rid of 'that girl,' as you say, for my aunt is as deluded about her as Ned and Bella, and she really does get the child along splendidly. Dispatch Ned, and then she can do no harm," said Lucia, watching Coventry's altered face as he stood in the moonlight, just outside the window where she sat.

"Have you no fears for me?" he asked smiling, as if ashamed of his momentary petulance.

"No, have you for yourself?" And a shade of anxiety passed over her face.

"I defy the Scotch witch to enchant me, except with her music," he added, moving down the terrace again, for Jean was singing like a nightingale.

As the song ended, he put aside the curtain, and said, abruptly, "Has anyone any commands for London? I am going there tomorrow."

"A pleasant trip to you," said Ned carelessly, though usually his brother's movements interested him extremely.

"I want quantities of things, but I must ask Mamma first." And Bella began to make a list.

"May I trouble you with a letter, Mr. Coventry?"

Jean Muir turned around on the music stool and looked at him with the cold keen glance which always puzzled him.

He bowed, saying, as if to them all, "I shall be off by the early train, so you must give me your orders tonight."

"Then come away, Ned, and leave Jean to write her letter."

And Bella took her reluctant brother from the room.

"I will give you the letter in the morning," said Miss Muir, with a curious quiver in her voice, and the look of one who forcibly suppressed some strong emotion.

"As you please." And Coventry went back to Lucia, wondering who Miss Muir was going to write to. He said nothing to his brother of the purpose which took him to town, lest a word should produce the catastrophe which he hoped to prevent; and Ned, who now lived in a sort of dream, seemed to forget Gerald's existence altogether.

With unwonted energy Coventry was astir seven next morning. Lucia gave him his breakfast, and as he left the room to order the carriage, Miss Muir came gliding downstairs, very pale and heavy-eyed (with a sleepless, tearful night, he thought) and, putting a delicate little letter into his hand, said hurriedly, "Please leave this at Lady Sydney's, and if you see her, say 'I have remembered.'"

Her peculiar manner and peculiar message struck him. His eye involuntarily glanced at the address of the letter and read young Sydney's name. Then, conscious of his mistake, he thrust it into his pocket with a hasty "Good morning," and left Miss Muir standing with one hand pressed on her heart, the other half extended as if to recall the letter.

All the way to London, Coventry found it impossible to forget the almost tragical expression of the girl's face, and it haunted him through the bustle of two busy days. Ned's affair was put in the way of being speedily accomplished, Bella's commissions were executed, his mother's pet delicacies provided for her, and a gift for Lucia, whom the family had given him for his future mate, as he was too lazy to choose for himself.

Jean Muir's letter he had not delivered, for Lady Sydney was in the country and her townhouse closed. Curious to see how she would receive his tidings, he went quietly in on his arrival at home. Everyone had dispersed to dress for dinner except Miss Muir, who was in the garden, the servant said.

"Very well, I have a message for her"; and, turning, the "young master," as they called him, went to seek her. In a remote corner he saw her sitting alone, buried in thought. As his step roused her, a look of surprise, followed by one of satisfaction, passed over her face, and, rising, she beckoned to him with an almost eager gesture. Much amazed, he went to her and offered the letter, saying kindly, "I regret that I could not deliver it. Lady Sydney is in the country, and I did not like to post it without your leave. Did I do right?"

"Quite right, thank you very much—it is better so." And with an air of relief, she tore the letter to atoms, and scattered them to the wind.

More amazed than ever, the young man was about to leave her when she said, with a mixture of entreaty and command, "Please stay a moment. I want to speak to you."

He paused, eyeing her with visible surprise, for a sudden color dyed her cheeks, and her lips trembled. Only for a moment, then she was quite self-possessed again. Motioning him to the seat she had left, she remained standing while she said, in a low, rapid tone full of pain and of decision:

"Mr. Coventry, as the head of the house I want to speak to you, rather than to your mother, of a most unhappy affair which has occurred during your absence. My month of probation ends today; your mother wishes me to remain; I, too, wish it sincerely, for I am happy here, but I ought not. Read this, and you will see why."

She put a hastily written note into his hand and watched him intently while he read it. She saw him flush with anger, bite his lips, and knit his brows, then assume his haughtiest look, as he lifted his eyes and said in his most sarcastic tone, "Very well for a beginning. The boy has eloquence. Pity that it should be wasted. May I ask if you have replied to this rhapsody?"

"I have."

"And what follows? He begs you 'to fly with him, to share his fortunes, and be the good angel of his life.' Of course you consent?"

There was no answer, for, standing erect before him, Miss Muir regarded him with an expression of proud patience, like one who expected reproaches, yet was too generous to resent them. Her manner had its effect. Dropping his bitter tone, Coventry asked briefly, "Why do you show me this? What can I do?"

"I show it that you may see how much in earnest 'the boy' is, and how open I desire to be. You can control, advise, and comfort your brother, and help me to see what is my duty."

"You love him?" demanded Coventry bluntly.

"No!" was the quick, decided answer.

"Then why make him love you?"

"I never tried to do it. Your sister will testify that I have endeavored to avoid him as I—" And he finished the sentence with an unconscious tone of pique, "As you have avoided me."

She bowed silently, and he went on:

"I will do you the justice to say that nothing can be more blameless than your conduct toward myself; but why allow Ned to haunt you evening after evening? What could you expect of a romantic boy who had nothing to do but lose his heart to the first attractive woman he met?"

A momentary glisten shone in Jean Muir's steel-blue eyes as the last words left the young man's lips; but it was gone instantly, and her voice was full of reproach, as she said, steadily, impulsively, "If the 'romantic boy' had been allowed to lead the life of a man, as he longed to do, he would have had no time to lose his heart to the first sorrowful girl whom he pitied. Mr. Coventry, the fault is yours. Do not blame your brother, but generously own your mistake and retrieve it in the speediest, kindest manner."

For an instant Gerald sat dumb. Never since his father died had anyone reproved him; seldom in his life had he been blamed. It was a new experience, and the very novelty added to the effect. He saw his fault, regretted it, and admired the brave sincerity of the girl in telling him of it. But he did not know how to deal with the case, and was forced to confess not only past negligence but present incapacity. He was as honorable as he was proud, and with an effort he said frankly, "You are right, Miss Muir. I *am* to blame, yet as soon as I saw the danger, I tried to avert it. My visit to town was on Ned's account; he will have his commission very soon, and then he will be sent out of harm's way. Can I do more?"

"No, it is too late to send him away with a free and happy heart. He must bear his pain as he can, and it may help to make a man of him," she said sadly.

"He'll soon forget," began Coventry, who found the thought of gay Ned suffering an uncomfortable one.

"Yes, thank heaven, that is possible, for men."

Miss Muir pressed her hands together, with a dark expression on her half-averted face. Something in her tone, her manner, touched Coventry; he fancied that some old wound bled, some bitter memory awoke at the approach of a new lover. He was young, heart-whole, and romantic, under all his cool nonchalance of manner. This girl, who he fancied loved his friend and who was beloved by his brother, became an object of interest to him. He pitied her, desired to help her, and regretted his past distrust, as a chivalrous man always regrets injustice to a woman. She was happy here, poor, homeless soul, and she should stay. Bella loved her, his mother took comfort in her, and when Ned was gone, no one's peace would be endangered by her winning ways, her rich accomplishments. These thoughts swept through his mind during a brief pause, and when he spoke, it was to say gently:

"Miss Muir, I thank you for the frankness which must have been painful to you, and I will do my best to be worthy of the confidence which you repose in me. You were both discreet and kind to speak only to me. This thing would have troubled my mother extremely, and have done no good. I shall see Ned, and try and repair my long neglect as promptly as possible. I know you will help me, and in return let me beg of you to remain, for he will soon be gone."

She looked at him with eyes full of tears, and there was no coolness in the voice that answered softly, "You are too kind, but I had better go; it is not wise to stay."

"Why not?"

She colored beautifully, hesitated, then spoke out in the clear, steady voice which was her greatest charm, "If I had known there were sons in this family, I never should have come. Lady Sydney spoke only of your sister, and when I found two gentlemen, I was troubled, because—I am so unfortunate—or rather, people are so kind as to like me more than I deserve. I thought I could stay a month, at least, as your brother spoke of going away, and you were already affianced, but—"

"I am not affianced."

Why he said that, Coventry could not tell, but the words passed his lips hastily and could not be recalled. Jean Muir took the announcement oddly enough. She shrugged her shoulders with an air of extreme annoyance, and said almost rudely, "Then you should be; you will be soon. But that is nothing to me. Miss Beaufort wishes me gone, and I am too proud to remain and become the cause of disunion in a happy family. No, I will go, and go at once."

She turned away impetuously, but Edward's arm detained her, and Edward's voice demanded, tenderly, "Where will you go, my Jean?"

The tender touch and name seemed to rob her of her courage and calmness, for, leaning on her lover, she hid her face and sobbed audibly.

"Now don't make a scene, for heaven's sake," began Coventry impatiently, as his brother eyed him fiercely, divining at once what had passed, for his letter was still in Gerald's hand and Jean's last words had reached her lover's ear.

"Who gave you the right to read that, and to interfere in my affairs?" demanded Edward hotly.

"Miss Muir" was the reply, as Coventry threw away the paper.

"And you add to the insult by ordering her out of the house," cried Ned with increasing wrath.

"On the contrary, I beg her to remain."

"The deuce you do! And why?"

"Because she is useful and happy here, and I am unwilling that your folly should rob her of a home which she likes."

"You are very thoughtful and devoted all at once, but I beg you will not trouble yourself. Jean's happiness and home will be my care now."

"My dear boy, do be reasonable. The thing is impossible. Miss Muir sees it herself; she came to tell me, to ask how best to arrange matters without troubling my mother. I've been to town to attend to your affairs, and you may be off now very soon."

"I have no desire to go. Last month it was the wish of my heart. Now I'll accept nothing from you." And Edward turned moodily away from his brother.

"What folly! Ned, you *must* leave home. It is all arranged and cannot be given up now. A change is what you need, and it will make a man of you. We shall miss you, of course, but you will be where you'll see something of life, and that is better for you than getting into mischief here."

"Are you going away, Jean?" asked Edward, ignoring his brother entirely and bending over the girl, who still hid her face and wept. She did not speak, and Gerald answered for her.

"No, why should she if you are gone?"

"Do you mean to stay?" asked the lover eagerly of Jean.

"I wish to remain, but—" She paused and looked up. Her eyes went from one face to the other, and she added, decidedly, "Yes, I must go, it is not wise to stay even when you are gone."

Neither of the young men could have explained why that hurried glance affected them as it did, but each felt conscious of a willful desire to oppose the other. Edward suddenly felt that his brother loved Miss Muir, and was bent on removing her from his way. Gerald had a vague idea that Miss Muir feared to remain on his account, and he longed to show her that he was quite safe. Each felt angry, and each showed it in a different way, one being violent, the other satirical.

"You are right, Jean, this is not the place for you; and you must let me see you in a safer home before I go," said Ned, significantly.

"It strikes me that this will be a particularly safe home when your dangerous self is removed," began Coventry, with an aggravating smile of calm superiority.

"And *I* think that I leave a more dangerous person than myself behind me, as poor Lucia can testify."

"Be careful what you say, Ned, or I shall be forced to remind you that I am master here. Leave Lucia's name out of this disagreeable affair, if you please."

"You *are* master here, but not of me, or my actions, and you have no right to expect obedience or respect, for you inspire neither. Jean, I asked you to go with me secretly; now I ask you openly to share my fortune. In my brother's presence I ask, and *will* have an answer."

He caught her hand impetuously, with a defiant look at Coventry, who still smiled, as if at boy's play, though his eyes were kindling and his face changing with the still, white wrath which is more terrible than any sudden outburst. Miss Muir looked frightened; she shrank away from her passionate young lover, cast an appealing glance at Gerald, and seemed as if she longed to claim his protection yet dared not.

"Speak!" cried Edward, desperately. "Don't look to him, tell me truly, with your own lips, do you, can you love me, Jean?"

"I have told you once. Why pain me by forcing another hard reply," she said pitifully, still shrinking from his grasp and seeming to appeal to his brother.

"You wrote a few lines, but I'll not be satisfied with that. You shall answer; I've seen love in your eyes, heard it in your voice, and I know it is hidden in your heart. You fear to own it; do not hesitate, no one can part us—speak, Jean, and satisfy me."

Drawing her hand decidedly away, she went a step nearer Coventry, and answered, slowly, distinctly, though her lips trembled, and she evidently dreaded the effect of her words, "I will speak, and speak truly. You have seen love in my face; it is in my heart, and I do not hesitate to own it, cruel as it is to force the truth from me, but this love is not for you. Are you satisfied?"

He looked at her with a despairing glance and stretched his hand toward her beseechingly. She seemed to fear a blow, for suddenly she clung to Gerald with a faint cry. The act, the look of fear, the protecting gesture Coventry involuntarily made were too much for Edward, already excited by conflicting passions. In a paroxysm of blind wrath, he caught up a large pruning knife left there by the gardener, and would have dealt his brother a fatal blow had he not warded it off with his arm. The stroke fell, and another might have followed had not Miss Muir with unexpected courage and strength wrested the knife from Edward and flung it into the little pond near by. Coventry dropped down upon the seat, for the blood poured from a deep wound in his arm, showing by its rapid flow that an artery had been severed. Edward stood aghast, for with the blow his fury passed, leaving him overwhelmed with remorse and shame.

Gerald looked up at him, smiled faintly, and said, with no sign of reproach or anger, "Never mind, Ned. Forgive and forget. Lend me a hand to the house, and don't disturb anyone. It's not much, I dare say." But his lips whitened as he spoke, and his strength failed him. Edward sprang to support him, and Miss Muir, forgetting her terrors, proved herself a girl of uncommon skill and courage.

"Quick! Lay him down. Give me your handkerchief, and bring some water," she said, in a tone of quiet command. Poor Ned obeyed and watched her with breathless suspense while she tied the handkerchief tightly around the arm, thrust the handle of his riding whip underneath, and pressed it firmly above the severed artery to stop the dangerous flow of blood.

"Dr. Scott is with your mother, I think. Go and bring him here" was the next order; and Edward darted away, thankful to do anything to ease the terror which possessed him. He was gone some minutes, and while they waited Coventry watched the girl as she knelt beside him, bathing his face with one hand while with the other she held the bandage firmly in its place. She was pale, but quite steady and self-possessed, and her eyes shone with a strange brilliancy as she looked down at him. Once, meeting his look of grateful wonder, she smiled a reassuring smile that made her lovely, and said, in a soft, sweet tone never used to him before, "Be quiet. There is no danger. I will stay by you till help comes."

Help did come speedily, and the doctor's first words were "Who improvised that tourniquet?"

"She did," murmured Coventry.

"Then you may thank her for saving your life. By Jove! It was capitally done"; and the old doctor looked at the girl with as much admiration as curiosity in his face.

"Never mind that. See to the wound, please, while I ran for bandages, and salts, and wine."

Miss Muir was gone as she spoke, so fleetly that it was in vain to call her back or catch her. During her brief absence, the story was told by repentant Ned and the wound examined.

"Fortunately I have my case of instruments with me," said the doctor, spreading on the bench a long array of tiny, glittering implements of torture. "Now, Mr. Ned, come here, and hold the arm in that way, while I tie the artery. Hey! That will never do. Don't tremble so, man, look away and hold it steadily."

"I can't!" And poor Ned turned faint and white, not at the sight but with the bitter thought that he had longed to kill his brother.

"I will hold it," and a slender white hand lifted the bare and bloody arm so firmly, steadily, that Coventry sighed a sigh of relief, and Dr. Scott fell to work with an emphatic nod of approval.

It was soon over, and while Edward ran in to bid the servants beware of alarming their mistress, Dr. Scott put up his instruments and Miss Muir used salts, water, and wine so skillfully that Gerald was able to walk to his room, leaning on the old man, while the girl supported the wounded arm, as no sling could be made on the spot. As he entered the chamber, Coventry turned, put out his left hand, and with much feeling in his fine eyes said simply, "Miss Muir, I thank you."

The color came up beautifully in her pale cheeks as she pressed the hand and without a word vanished from the room. Lucia and the housekeeper came bustling in, and there was no lack of attendance on the invalid. He soon wearied of it, and sent them all away but Ned, who remorsefully haunted the chamber, looking like a comely young Cain and feeling like an outcast.

"Come here, lad, and tell me all about it. I was wrong to be domineering. Forgive me, and believe that I care for your happiness more sincerely than for my own."

These frank and friendly words healed the breach between the two brothers and completely conquered Ned. Gladly did he relate his love passages, for no young lover ever tires of that amusement if he has a sympathizing auditor, and Gerald *was* sympathetic now. For an hour did he lie listening patiently to the history of the growth of his brother's passion. Emotion gave the narrator eloquence, and Jean Muir's character was painted in glowing colors. All her unsuspected kindness to those about her was dwelt upon; all her faithful care, her sisterly interest in Bella, her gentle attentions to their mother, her sweet forbearance with Lucia, who plainly showed her dislike, and most of all, her friendly counsel, sympathy, and regard for Ned himself.

"She would make a man of me. She puts strength and courage into me as no one else can. She is unlike any girl I ever saw; there's no sentimentality about her; she is wise, and kind, and sweet. She says what she means, looks you straight in the eye, and is as true as steel. I've tried her, I know her, and—ah, Gerald, I love her so!"

Here the poor lad leaned his face into his hands and sighed a sigh that made his brother's heart ache.

"Upon my soul, Ned, I feel for you; and if there was no obstacle on her part, I'd do my best for you. She loves Sydney, and so there is nothing for it but to bear your fate like a man."

"Are you sure about Sydney? May it not be some one else?" and Ned eyed his brother with a suspicious look.

Coventry told him all he knew and surmised concerning his friend, not forgetting the letter. Edward mused a moment, then seemed relieved, and said frankly, "I'm glad it's Sydney and not you. I can bear it better."

"Me!" ejaculated Gerald, with a laugh.

"Yes, you; I've been tormented lately with a fear that you cared for her, or rather, she for you."

"You jealous young fool! We never see or speak to one another scarcely, so how could we get up a tender interest?"

"What do you lounge about on that terrace for every evening? And why does she get fluttered when your shadow begins to come and go?" demanded Edward.

"I like the music and don't care for the society of the singer, that's why I walk there. The fluttering is all your imagination; Miss Muir isn't a woman to be fluttered by a man's shadow." And Coventry glanced at his useless arm.

"Thank you for that, and for not saying 'little Muir,' as you generally do. Perhaps it was my imagination. But she never makes fun of you now, and so I fancied she might have lost her heart to the 'young master.' Women often do, you know."

"She used to ridicule me, did she?" asked Coventry, taking no notice of the latter part of his brother's speech, which was quite true nevertheless.

"Not exactly, she was too well-bred for that. But sometimes when Bella and I joked about you, she'd say something so odd or witty that it was irresistible. You're used to being laughed at, so you don't mind, I know, just among ourselves."

"Not I. Laugh away as much as you like," said Gerald. But he did mind, and wanted exceedingly to know what Miss Muir had said, yet was too proud to ask. He turned restlessly and uttered a sigh of pain.

"I'm talking too much; it's bad for you. Dr. Scott said you must be quiet. Now go to sleep, if you can."

Edward left the bedside but not the room, for he would let no one take his place. Coventry tried to sleep, found it impossible, and after a restless hour called his brother back.

"If the bandage was loosened a bit, it would ease my arm and then I could sleep. Can you do it, Ned?"

"I dare not touch it. The doctor gave orders to leave it till he came in the morning, and I shall only do harm if I try."

"But I tell you it's too tight. My arm is swelling and the pain is intense. It can't be right to leave it so. Dr. Scott dressed it in a hurry and did it too tight. Common sense will tell you that," said Coventry impatiently.

"I'll call Mrs. Morris; she will understand what's best to be done." And Edward moved toward the door, looking anxious.

"Not she, she'll only make a stir and torment me with her chatter. I'll bear it as long as I can, and perhaps Dr. Scott will come tonight. He said he would if possible. Go to your dinner, Ned. I can ring for Neal if I need anything. I shall sleep if I'm alone, perhaps."

Edward reluctantly obeyed, and his brother was left to himself. Little rest did he find, however, for the pain of the wounded arm grew unbearable, and, taking a sudden resolution, he rang for his servant.

"Neal, go to Miss Coventry's study, and if Miss Muir is there, ask her to be kind enough to come to me. I'm in great pain, and she understand wounds better than anyone else in the house."

With much surprise in his face, the man departed and a few moments after the door noiselessly opened and Miss Muir came in. It had been a very warm day, and for the first time she had left off her plain black dress. All in white, with no ornament but her fair hair, and a fragrant posy of violets in her belt, she looked a different woman from the meek, nunlike creature one usually saw about the house. Her face was as altered as her dress, for now a soft color glowed in her cheeks, her eyes smiled shyly, and her lips no longer wore the firm look of one who forcibly repressed every emotion. A fresh, gentle, and charming woman she seemed, and Coventry found the dull room suddenly brightened by her presence. Going straight to him, she said simply, and with a happy, helpful look very comforting to see, "I'm glad you sent for me. What can I do for you?"

He told her, and before the complaint was ended, she began loosening the bandages with the decision of one who understood what was to be done and had faith in herself.

"Ah, that's relief, that's comfort!" ejaculated Coventry, as the last tight fold fell away. "Ned was afraid I should bleed to death if he touched me. What will the doctor say to us?"

"I neither know nor care. I shall say to him that he is a bad surgeon to bind it so closely, and not leave orders to have it untied if necessary. Now I shall make it easy and put you to sleep, for that is what you need. Shall I? May I?"

"I wish you would, if you can."

And while she deftly rearranged the bandages, the young man watched her curiously. Presently he asked, "How came you to know so much about these things?"

"In the hospital where I was ill, I saw much that interested me, and when I got better, I used to sing to the patients sometimes."

"Do you mean to sing to me?" he asked, in the submissive tone men unconsciously adopt when ill and in a woman's care.

"If you like it better than reading aloud in a dreamy tone," she answered, as she tied the last knot.

"I do, much better," he said decidedly.

"You are feverish. I shall wet your forehead, and then you will be quite comfortable." She moved about the room in the quiet way which made it a pleasure to watch her, and, having mingled a little cologne with water, bathed his face as unconcernedly as if he had been a child. Her proceedings not only comforted but amused Coventry, who mentally contrasted her with the stout, beer-drinking matron who had ruled over him in his last illness.

"A clever, kindly little woman," he thought, and felt quite at his ease, she was so perfectly easy herself.

"There, now you look more like yourself," she said with an approving nod as she finished, and smoothed the dark locks off his forehead with a cool, soft hand. Then seating herself in a large chair near by, she began to sing, while tidily rolling up the fresh bandages which had been left for the morning. Coventry lay watching her by the dim light that burned in the room, and she sang on as easily as a bird, a dreamy, low-toned lullaby, which soothed the listener like a spell. Presently, looking up to see the effect of her song, she found the young man wide awake, and regarding her with a curious mixture of pleasure, interest, and admiration.

"Shut your eyes, Mr. Coventry," she said, with a reproving shake of the head, and an odd little smile.

He laughed and obeyed, but could not resist an occasional covert glance from under his lashes at the slender white figure in the great velvet chair. She saw him and frowned.

"You are very disobedient; why won't you sleep?"

"I can't, I want to listen. I'm fond of nightingales."

"Then I shall sing no more, but try something that has never failed yet. Give me your hand, please."

Much amazed, he gave it, and, taking it in both her small ones, she sat down behind the curtain and remained as mute and motionless as a statue. Coventry smiled to himself at first, and wondered which would tire first. But soon a subtle warmth seemed to steal from the soft palms that enclosed his own, his heart beat quicker, his breath grew unequal, and a thousand fancies danced through his brain. He sighed, and said dreamily, as he turned his face toward her, "I like this." And in the act of speaking, seemed to sink into a soft cloud which encompassed him about with an atmosphere of perfect repose. More than this he could not remember, for sleep, deep and dreamless, fell upon him, and when he woke, daylight was shining in between the curtains, his hand lay alone on the coverlet, and his fair-haired enchantress was gone.

CHAPTER IV

A DISCOVERY

For several days Coventry was confined to his room, much against his will, though everyone did their best to lighten his irksome captivity. His mother petted him, Bella sang, Lucia read, Edward was devoted, and all the household, with one exception, were eager to serve the young master. Jean Muir never came near him, and Jean Muir alone seemed to possess the power of amusing him. He soon tired of the others, wanted something new; recalled the piquant character of the girl and took a fancy into his head that she would lighten his ennui. After some hesitation, he carelessly spoke of her to Bella, but nothing came of it, for Bella only said Jean was well, and very busy doing something lovely to surprise Mamma with. Edward complained that he never saw her, and Lucia ignored her existence altogether. The only intelligence the invalid received was from the gossip of two housemaids over their work in the next room. From them he learned that the governess had been "scolded" by Miss Beaufort for going to Mr. Coventry's room; that she had taken it very sweetly and kept herself carefully out of the way of both young gentlemen, though it was plain to see that Mr. Ned was dying for her.

Mr. Gerald amused himself by thinking over this gossip, and quite annoyed his sister by his absence of mind.

"Gerald, do you know Ned's commission has come?"

"Very interesting. Read on, Bella."

"You stupid boy! You don't know a word I say," and she put down the book to repeat her news.

"I'm glad of it; now we must get him off as soon as possible—that is, I suppose he will want to be off as soon as possible." And Coventry woke up from his reverie.

"You needn't check yourself, I know all about it. I think Ned was very foolish, and that Miss Muir has behaved beautifully. It's quite impossible, of course, but I wish it wasn't, I do so like to watch lovers. You and Lucia are so cold you are not a bit interesting."

"You'll do me a favor if you'll stop all that nonsense about Lucia and me. We are not lovers, and never shall be, I fancy. At all events, I'm tired of the thing, and wish you and Mamma would let it drop, for the present at least."

"Oh Gerald, you know Mamma has set her heart upon it, that Papa desired it, and poor Lucia loves you so much. How can you speak of dropping what will make us all so happy?"

"It won't make me happy, and I take the liberty of thinking that this is of some importance. I'm not bound in any way, and don't intend to be till I am ready. Now we'll talk about Ned."

Much grieved and surprised, Bella obeyed, and devoted herself to Edward, who very wisely submitted to his fate and prepared to leave home for some months. For a week the house was in a state of excitement about his departure, and everyone but Jean was busied for him. She was scarcely seen; every morning she gave Bella her lessons, every afternoon drove out with Mrs. Coventry, and nearly every evening went up to the Hall to read to Sir John, who found his wish granted without exactly knowing how it had been done.

The day Edward left, he came down from bidding his mother good-bye, looking very pale, for he had lingered in his sister's little room with Miss Muir as long as he dared.

"Good-bye, dear. Be kind to Jean," he whispered as he kissed his sister.

"I will, I will," returned Bella, with tearful eyes.

"Take care of Mamma, and remember Lucia," he said again, as he touched his cousin's beautiful cheek.

"Fear nothing. I will keep them apart," she whispered back, and Coventry heard it.

Edward offered his hand to his brother, saying, significantly, as he looked him in the eye, "I trust you, Gerald."

"You may, Ned."

Then he went, and Coventry tired himself with wondering what Lucia meant. A few days later he understood.

Now Ned is gone, little Muir will appear, I fancy, he said to himself; but "little Muir" did not appear, and seemed to shun him more carefully than she had done her lover. If he went to the drawing room in the evening hoping for music, Lucia alone was there. If he tapped at Bella's door, there was always a pause before she opened it, and no sign of Jean appeared though her voice had been audible when he knocked. If he went to the library, a hasty rustle and the sound of flying feet betrayed that the room was deserted at his approach. In the garden Miss Muir never failed to avoid him, and if by chance they met in hall or breakfast room, she passed him with downcast eyes and the briefest, coldest greeting. All this annoyed him intensely, and the more she eluded him, the more he desired to see her—from a spirit of opposition, he said, nothing more. It fretted and yet it entertained him, and he found a lazy sort of pleasure in thwarting the girl's little maneuvers. His patience gave out at last, and he resolved to know what was the meaning of this peculiar conduct. Having locked and taken away the key of one door in the library, he waited till Miss Muir went in to get a book for his uncle. He had heard her speak to Bella of it, knew that she believed him with his mother, and smiled to himself as he stole after her. She was standing in a chair, reaching up, and he had time to see a slender waist, a pretty foot, before he spoke.

"Can I help you, Miss Muir?"

She started, dropped several books, and turned scarlet, as she said hurriedly, "Thank you, no; I can get the steps."

"My long arm will be less trouble. I've got but one, and that is tired of being idle, so it is very much at your service. What will you have?"

"I—I—you startled me so I've forgotten." And Jean laughed, nervously, as she looked about her as if planning to escape.

"I beg your pardon, wait till you remember, and let me thank you for the enchanted sleep you gave me ten days ago. I've had no chance yet, you've shunned me so pertinaciously."

"Indeed I try not to be rude, but—" She checked herself, and turned her face away, adding, with an accent of pain in her voice, "It is not my fault, Mr. Coventry. I only obey orders."

"Whose orders?" he demanded, still standing so that she could not escape.

"Don't ask; it is one who has a right to command where you are concerned. Be sure that it is kindly meant, though it may seem folly to us. Nay, don't be angry, laugh at it, as I do, and let me run away, please."

She turned, and looked down at him with tears in her eyes, a smile on her lips, and an expression half sad, half arch, which was altogether charming. The frown passed from his face, but he still looked grave and said decidedly, "No one has a right to command in this house but my mother or myself. Was it she who bade you avoid me as if I was a madman or a pest?"

"Ah, don't ask. I promised not to tell, and you would not have me break my word, I know." And still smiling, she regarded him with a look of merry malice which made any other reply unnecessary. It was Lucia, he thought, and disliked his cousin intensely just then. Miss Muir moved as if to step down; he detained her, saying earnestly, yet with a smile, "Do you consider me the master here?"

"Yes," and to the word she gave a sweet, submissive intonation which made it expressive of the respect, regard, and confidence which men find pleasantest when women feel and show it. Unconsciously his face softened, and he looked up at her with a different glance from any he had ever given her before.

"Well, then, will you consent to obey me if I am not tyrannical or unreasonable in my demands?"

"I'll try."

"Good! Now frankly, I want to say that all this sort of thing is very disagreeable to me. It annoys me to be a restraint upon anyone's liberty or comfort, and I beg you will go and come as freely as you like, and not mind Lucia's absurdities. She means well, but hasn't a particle of penetration or tact. Will you promise this?"

"No."

"Why not?"

"It is better as it is, perhaps."

"But you called it folly just now."

"Yes, it seems so, and yet—" She paused, looking both confused and distressed.

Coventry lost patience, and said hastily, "You women are such enigmas I never expect to understand you! Well, I've done my best to make you comfortable, but if you prefer to lead this sort of life, I beg you will do so."

"I *don't* prefer it; it is hateful to me. I like to be myself, to have my liberty, and the confidence of those about me. But I cannot think it kind to disturb the peace of anyone, and so I try to obey. I've promised Bella to remain, but I will go rather than have another scene with Miss Beaufort or with you."

Miss Muir had burst out impetuously, and stood there with a sudden fire in her eyes, sudden warmth and spirit in her face and voice that amazed Coventry. She was angry, hurt, and haughty, and the change only made her more attractive, for not a trace of her former meek self remained. Coventry was electrified, and still more surprised when she added, imperiously, with a gesture as if to put him aside, "Hand me that book and move away. I wish to go."

He obeyed, even offered his hand, but she refused it, stepped lightly down, and went to the door. There she turned, and with the same indignant voice, the same kindling eyes and glowing cheeks, she said rapidly, "I know I have no right to speak in this way. I restrain myself as long as I can, but when I can bear no more, my true self breaks loose, and I defy everything. I am tired of being a cold, calm machine; it is impossible with an ardent nature like mine, and I shall try no longer. I cannot help it if people love me. I don't want their love. I only ask to be left in peace, and why I am tormented so I cannot see. I've neither beauty, money, nor rank, yet every foolish boy mistakes my frank interest for something warmer, and makes me miserable. It is my misfortune. Think of me what you will, but beware of me in time, for against my will I may do you harm."

Almost fiercely she had spoken, and with a warning gesture she hurried from the room, leaving the young man feeling as if a sudden thunder-gust had swept through the house. For several minutes he sat in the chair she left, thinking deeply. Suddenly he rose, went to his sister, and said, in his usual tone of indolent good nature, "Bella, didn't I hear Ned ask you to be kind to Miss Muir?"

"Yes, and I try to be, but she is so odd lately."

"Odd! How do you mean?"

"Why, she is either as calm and cold as a statue, or restless and queer; she cries at night, I know, and sighs sadly when she thinks I don't hear. Something is the matter."

"She frets for Ned perhaps," began Coventry.

"Oh dear, no; it's a great relief to her that he is gone. I'm afraid that she likes someone very much, and someone don't like her. Can it be Mr. Sydney?"

"She called him a 'titled fool' once, but perhaps that didn't mean anything. Did you ever ask her about him?" said Coventry, feeling rather ashamed of his curiosity, yet unable to resist the temptation of questioning unsuspecting Bella.

"Yes, but she only looked at me in her tragical way, and said, so pitifully, 'My little friend, I hope you will never have to pass through the scenes I've passed through, but keep your peace unbroken all your life.' After that I dared say no more. I'm very fond of her, I want to make her happy, but I don't know how. Can you propose anything?"

"I was going to propose that you make her come among us more, now Ned is gone. It must be dull for her, moping about alone. I'm sure it is for me. She is an entertaining little person, and I enjoy her music very much. It's good for Mamma to have gay evenings; so you bestir yourself, and see what you can do for the general good of the family."

"That's all very charming, and I've proposed it more than once, but Lucia spoils all my plans. She is afraid you'll follow Ned's example, and that is so silly."

"Lucia is a—no, I won't say fool, because she has sense enough when she chooses; but I wish you'd just settle things with Mamma, and then Lucia can do nothing but submit," said Gerald angrily.

"I'll try, but she goes up to read to Uncle, you know, and since he has had the gout, she stays later, so I see little of her in the evening. There she goes now. I think she will captivate the old one as well as the young one, she is so devoted."

Coventry looked after her slender black figure, just vanishing through the great gate, and an uncomfortable fancy took possession of him, born of Bella's careless words. He sauntered away, and after eluding his cousin, who seemed looking for him, he turned toward the Hall, saying to himself, I will see what is going on up here. Such things have happened. Uncle is the simplest soul alive, and if the girl is ambitious, she can do what she will with him.

Here a servant came running after him and gave him a letter, which he thrust into his pocket without examining it. When he reached the Hall, he went quietly to his uncle's study. The door was ajar, and looking in, he saw a scene of tranquil comfort, very pleasant to watch. Sir John leaned in his easy chair with one foot on a cushion. He was dressed with his usual care and, in spite of the gout, looked like a handsome, well-preserved old gentleman. He was smiling as he listened, and his eyes rested complacently on Jean Muir, who sat near him reading in her musical voice, while the sunshine glittered on her hair and the soft rose of her cheek. She read well, yet Coventry thought her heart was not in her task, for once when she paused, while Sir John spoke, her eyes had an absent expression, and she leaned her head upon her hand, with an air of patient weariness.

Poor girl! I did her great injustice; she has no thought of captivating the old man, but amuses him from simple kindness. She is tired. I'll put an end to her task; and Coventry entered without knocking.

Sir John received him with an air of polite resignation, Miss Muir with a perfectly expressionless face.

"Mother's love, and how are you today, sir?"

"Comfortable, but dull, so I want you to bring the girls over this evening, to amuse the old gentleman. Mrs. King has got out the antique costumes and trumpery, as I promised Bella she should have them, and tonight we are to have a merrymaking, as we used to do when Ned was here."

"Very well, sir, I'll bring them. We've all been out of sorts since the lad left, and a little jollity will do us good. Are you going back, Miss Muir?" asked Coventry.

"No, I shall keep her to give me my tea and get things ready. Don't read anymore, my dear, but go and amuse yourself with the pictures, or whatever you like," said Sir John; and like a dutiful daughter she obeyed, as if glad to get away.

"That's a very charming girl, Gerald," began Sir John as she left the room. "I'm much interested in her, both on her own account and on her mother's."

"Her mother's! What do you know of her mother?" asked Coventry, much surprised.

"Her mother was Lady Grace Howard, who ran away with a poor Scotch minister twenty years ago. The family cast her off, and she lived and died so obscurely that very little is known of her except that she left an orphan girl at some small French pension. This is the girl, and a fine girl, too. I'm surprised that you did not know this."

"So am I, but it is like her not to tell. She is a strange, proud creature. Lady Howard's daughter! Upon my word, that is a discovery," and Coventry felt his interest in his sister's governess much increased by this fact; for, like all wellborn Englishmen, he valued rank and gentle blood even more than he cared to own.

"She has had a hard life of it, this poor little girl, but she has a brave spirit, and will make her way anywhere," said Sir John admiringly.

"Did Ned know this?" asked Gerald suddenly.

"No, she only told me yesterday. I was looking in the *Peerage* and chanced to speak of the Howards. She forgot herself and called Lady Grace her mother. Then I got the whole story, for the lonely little thing was glad to make a confidant of someone."

"That accounts for her rejection of Sydney and Ned: she knows she is their equal and will not snatch at the rank which is hers by right. No, she's not mercenary or ambitious."

"What do you say?" asked Sir John, for Coventry had spoken more to himself than to his uncle.

"I wonder if Lady Sydney was aware of this?" was all Gerald's answer.

"No, Jean said she did not wish to be pitied, and so told nothing to the mother. I think the son knew, but that was a delicate point, and I asked no questions."

"I shall write to him as soon as I discover his address. We have been so intimate I can venture to make a few inquiries about Miss Muir, and prove the truth of her story."

"Do you mean to say that you doubt it?" demanded Sir John angrily.

"I beg your pardon, Uncle, but I must confess I have an instinctive distrust of that young person. It is unjust, I dare say, yet I cannot banish it."

"Don't annoy me by expressing it, if you please. I have some penetration and experience, and I respect and pity Miss Muir heartily. This dislike of yours may be the cause of her late melancholy, hey, Gerald?" And Sir John looked suspiciously at his nephew.

Anxious to avert the rising storm, Coventry said hastily as he turned away, "I've neither time nor inclination to discuss the matter now, sir, but will be careful not to offend again. I'll take your message to Bella, so good-bye for an hour, Uncle."

And Coventry went his way through the park, thinking within himself, The dear old gentleman is getting fascinated, like poor Ned. How the deuce does the girl do it? Lady Howard's daughter, yet never told us; I don't understand that.

CHAPTER V

HOW THE GIRL DID IT

At home he found a party of young friends, who hailed with delight the prospect of a revel at the Hall. An hour later, the blithe company trooped into the great saloon, where preparations had already been made for a dramatic evening.

Good Sir John was in his element, for he was never so happy as when his house was full of young people. Several persons were chosen, and in a few moments the curtains were withdrawn from the first of these impromptu tableaux. A swarthy, darkly bearded man lay asleep on a tiger skin, in the shadow of a tent. Oriental arms and drapery surrounded him; an antique silver lamp burned dimly on a table where fruit lay heaped in costly dishes, and wine shone redly in half-emptied goblets. Bending over the sleeper was a woman robed with barbaric splendor. One hand turned back the embroidered sleeve from the arm which held a scimitar; one slender foot in a scarlet sandal was visible under the white tunic; her purple mantle swept down from snowy shoulders; fillets of gold bound her hair, and jewels shone on neck and arms. She was looking over her shoulder toward the entrance of the tent, with a steady yet stealthy look, so effective that for a moment the spectators held their breath, as if they also heard a passing footstep.

"Who is it?" whispered Lucia, for the face was new to her.

"Jean Muir," answered Coventry, with an absorbed look.

"Impossible! She is small and fair," began Lucia, but a hasty "Hush, let me look!" from her cousin silenced her.

Impossible as it seemed, he was right nevertheless; for Jean Muir it was. She had darkened her skin, painted her eyebrows, disposed some wild black locks over her fair hair, and thrown such an intensity of expression into her eyes that they darkened and dilated till they were as fierce as any southern eyes that ever flashed. Hatred, the deepest and bitterest, was written on her sternly beautiful face, courage glowed in her glance, power spoke in the nervous grip of the slender hand that held the weapon, and the indomitable will of the woman was expressed—even the firm pressure of the little foot half hidden in the tiger skin.

"Oh, isn't she splendid?" cried Bella under her breath.

"She looks as if she'd use her sword well when the time comes," said someone admiringly.

"Good night to Holofernes; his fate is certain," added another.

"He is the image of Sydney, with that beard on."

"Doesn't she look as if she really hated him?"

"Perhaps she does."

Coventry uttered the last exclamation, for the two which preceded it suggested an explanation of the marvelous change in Jean. It was not all art: the intense detestation mingled with a savage joy that the object of her hatred was in her power was too perfect to be feigned; and having the key to a part of her story, Coventry felt as if he caught a glimpse of the truth. It was but a glimpse, however, for the curtain dropped before he had half analyzed the significance of that strange face.

"Horrible! I'm glad it's over," said Lucia coldly.

"Magnificent! Encore! Encore!" cried Gerald enthusiastically.

But the scene was over, and no applause could recall the actress. Two or three graceful or gay pictures followed, but Jean was in none, and each lacked the charm which real talent lends to the simplest part.

"Coventry, you are wanted," called a voice. And to everyone's surprise, Coventry went, though heretofore he had always refused to exert himself when handsome actors were in demand.

"What part am I to spoil?" he asked, as he entered the green room, where several excited young gentlemen were costuming and attitudinizing.

"A fugitive cavalier. Put yourself into this suit, and lose no time asking questions. Miss Muir will tell you what to do. She is in the tableau, so no one will mind you," said the manager pro tem, throwing a rich old suit toward Coventry and resuming the painting of a moustache on his own boyish face.

A gallant cavalier was the result of Gerald's hasty toilet, and when he appeared before the ladies a general glance of admiration was bestowed upon him.

"Come along and be placed; Jean is ready on the stage." And Bella ran before him, exclaiming to her governess, "Here he is, quite splendid. Wasn't he good to do it?"

Miss Muir, in the charmingly prim and puritanical dress of a Roundhead damsel, was arranging some shrubs, but turned suddenly and dropped the green branch she held, as her eye met the glittering figure advancing toward her.

"You!" she said with a troubled look, adding low to Bella, "Why did you ask *him*? I begged you not."

"He is the only handsome man here, and the best actor if he likes. He won't play usually, so make the most of him." And Bella was off to finish powdering her hair for "The Marriage à la Mode."

"I was sent for and I came. Do you prefer some other person?" asked Coventry, at a loss to understand the half-anxious, half-eager expression of the face under the little cap.

It changed to one of mingled annoyance and resignation as she said, "It is too late. Please kneel here, half behind the shrubs; put down your hat, and—allow me—you are too elegant for a fugitive."

As he knelt before her, she disheveled his hair, pulled his lace collar awry, threw away his gloves and sword, and half untied the cloak that hung about his shoulders.

"That is better; your paleness is excellent—nay, don't spoil it. We are to represent the picture which hangs in the Hall. I need tell you no more. Now, Round-heads, place yourselves, and then ring up the curtain."

With a smile, Coventry obeyed her; for the picture was of two lovers, the young cavalier kneeling, with his arm around the waist of the girl, who tries to hide him with her little mantle, and presses his head to her bosom in an ecstasy of fear, as she glances back at the approaching pursuers. Jean hesitated an instant and shrank a little as his hand touched her; she blushed deeply, and her eyes fell before his. Then, as the bell rang, she threw herself into her part with sudden spirit. One arm half covered him with her cloak, the other pillowed his head on the muslin kerchief folded over her bosom, and she looked backward with such terror in her eyes that more than one chivalrous young spectator longed to hurry to the rescue. It lasted but a moment; yet in that moment Coventry experienced another new sensation. Many women had smiled on him, but he had remained heart-whole, cool, and careless, quite unconscious of the power which a woman possesses and knows how to use, for the weal or woe of man. Now, as he knelt there with a soft arm about him, a slender waist yielding to his touch, and a maiden heart throbbing against his cheek, for the first time in his life he felt the indescribable spell of womanhood, and looked the ardent lover to perfection. Just as his face assumed this new and most becoming aspect, the curtain dropped, and clamorous encores recalled him to the fact that Miss Muir was trying to escape from his hold, which had grown painful in its unconscious pressure. He sprang up, half bewildered, and looking as he had never looked before.

"Again! Again!" called Sir John. And the young men who played the Round-heads, eager to share in the applause begged for a repetition in new attitudes.

"A rustle has betrayed you, we have fired and shot the brave girl, and she lies dying, you know. That will be effective; try it, Miss Muir," said one. And with a long breath, Jean complied.

The curtain went up, showing the lover still on his knees, unmindful of the captors who clutched him by the shoulder, for at his feet the girl lay dying. Her head was on his breast, now, her eyes looked full into his, no longer wild with fear, but eloquent with the love which even death could not conquer. The power of those tender eyes thrilled Coventry with a strange delight, and set his heart beating as rapidly as hers had done. She felt his hands tremble, saw the color flash into his cheek, knew that she had touched him at last, and when she rose it was with a sense of triumph which she found it hard to conceal. Others thought it fine acting; Coventry tried to believe so; but Lucia set her teeth, and, as the curtain fell on that second picture, she left her place to hurry behind the scenes, bent on putting an end to such dangerous play. Several actors were complimenting the mimic lovers. Jean took it merrily, but Coventry, in spite of himself, betrayed that he was excited by something deeper than mere gratified vanity.

As Lucia appeared, his manner changed to its usual indifference; but he could not quench the unwonted fire of his eyes, or keep all trace of emotion out of his face, and she saw this with a sharp pang.

"I have come to offer my help. You must be tired, Miss Muir. Can I relieve you?" said Lucia hastily.

"Yes, thank you. I shall be very glad to leave the rest to you, and enjoy them from the front."

So with a sweet smile Jean tripped away, and to Lucia's dismay Coventry followed.

"I want you, Gerald; please stay," she cried.

"I've done my part—no more tragedy for me tonight." And he was gone before she could entreat or command.

There was no help for it; she must stay and do her duty, or expose her jealousy to the quick eyes about her. For a time she bore it; but the sight of her cousin leaning over the chair she had left and chatting with the governess, who now filled it, grew unbearable, and she dispatched a little girl with a message to Miss Muir.

"Please, Miss Beaufort wants you for Queen Bess, as you are the only lady with red hair. Will you come?" whispered the child, quite unconscious of any hidden sting in her words.

"Yes, dear, willingly though I'm not stately enough for Her Majesty, nor handsome enough," said Jean, rising with an untroubled face, though she resented the feminine insult.

"Do you want an Essex? I'm all dressed for it," said Coventry, following to the door with a wistful look.

"No, Miss Beaufort said *you* were not to come. She doesn't want you both together," said the child decidedly.

Jean gave him a significant look, shrugged her shoulders, and went away smiling her odd smile, while Coventry paced up and down the hall in a curious state of unrest, which made him forgetful of everything till the young people came gaily out to supper.

"Come, bonny Prince Charlie, take me down, and play the lover as charmingly as you did an hour ago. I never thought you had so much warmth in you," said Bella, taking his arm and drawing him on against his will.

"Don't be foolish, child. Where is—Lucia?"

Why he checked Jean's name on his lips and substituted another's, he could not tell; but a sudden shyness in speaking of her possessed him, and though he saw her nowhere, he would not ask for her. His cousin came down looking lovely in a classical costume; but Gerald scarcely saw her, and, when the merriment was at its height, he slipped away to discover what had become of Miss Muir.

Alone in the deserted drawing room he found her, and paused to watch her a moment before he spoke; for something in her attitude and face struck him. She was leaning wearily back in the great chair which had served for a throne. Her royal robes were still unchanged, though the crown was off and all her fair hair hung about her shoulders. Excitement and exertion made her brilliant, the rich dress became her wonderfully, and an air of luxurious indolence changed the meek governess into a charming woman. She leaned on the velvet cushions as if she were used to such support; she played with the jewels which had crowned her as carelessly as if she were born to wear them; her attitude was full of negligent grace, and the expression of her face half proud, half pensive, as if her thoughts were bittersweet.

One would know she was wellborn to see her now. Poor girl, what a burden a life of dependence must be to a spirit like hers! I wonder what she is thinking of so intently. And Coventry indulged in another look before he spoke.

"Shall I bring you some supper, Miss Muir?"

"Supper!" she ejaculated, with a start. "Who thinks of one's body when one's soul is—" She stopped there, knit her brows, and laughed faintly as she added, "No, thank you. I want nothing but advice, and that I dare not ask of anyone."

"Why not?"

"Because I have no right."

"Everyone has a right to ask help, especially the weak of the strong. Can I help you? Believe me, I most heartily offer my poor services."

"Ah, you forget! This dress, the borrowed splendor of these jewels, the freedom of this gay evening, the romance of the part you played, all blind you to the reality. For a moment I cease to be a servant, and for a moment you treat me as an equal."

It was true; he *had* forgotten. That soft, reproachful glance touched him, his distrust melted under the new charm, and he answered with real feeling in voice and face, "I treat you as an equal because you *are* one; and when I offered help, it is not to my sister's governess alone, but to Lady Howard's daughter."

"Who told you that?" she demanded, sitting erect.

"My uncle. Do not reproach him. It shall go no further, if you forbid it. Are you sorry that I know it?"

"Yes."

"Why?"

"Because I will not be pitied!" And her eyes flashed as she made a half-defiant gesture.

"Then, if I may not pity the hard fate which has befallen an innocent life, may I admire the courage which meets adverse fortune so bravely, and conquers the world by winning the respect and regard of all who see and honor it?"

Miss Muir averted her face, put up her hand, and answered hastily, "No, no, not that! Do not be kind; it destroys the only barrier now left between us. Be cold to me as before, forget what I am, and let me go on my way, unknown, unpitied, and unloved!"

Her voice faltered and failed as the last word was uttered, and she bent her face upon her hand. Something jarred upon Coventry in this speech, and moved him to say, almost rudely, "You need have no fears for me. Lucia will tell you what an iceberg I am."

"Then Lucia would tell me wrong. I have the fatal power of reading character; I know you better than she does, and I see—" There she stopped abruptly.

"What? Tell me and prove your skill," he said eagerly.

Turning, she fixed her eyes on him with a penetrating power that made him shrink as she said slowly, "Under the ice I see fire, and warn you to beware lest it prove a volcano."

For a moment he sat dumb, wondering at the insight of the girl; for she was the first to discover the hidden warmth of a nature too proud to confess its tender impulses, or the ambitions that slept till some potent voice awoke them. The blunt, almost stern manner in which she warned him away from her only made her more attractive; for there was no conceit or arrogance in it, only a foreboding fear emboldened by past suffering to be frank. Suddenly he spoke impetuously:

"You are right! I am not what I seem, and my indolent indifference is but the mask under which I conceal my real self. I could be as passionate, as energetic and aspiring as Ned, if I had any aim in life. I have none, and so I am what you once called me, a thing to pity and despise."

"I never said that!" cried Jean indignantly.

"Not in those words, perhaps; but you looked it and thought it, though you phrased it more mildly. I deserved it, but I shall deserve it no longer. I am beginning to wake from my disgraceful idleness, and long for some work that shall make a man of me. Why do you go? I annoy you with my confessions. Pardon me. They are the first I ever made; they shall be the last."

"No, oh no! I am too much honored by your confidence; but is it wise, is it loyal to tell *me* your hopes and aims? Has not Miss Beaufort the first right to be your confidante?"

Coventry drew back, looking intensely annoyed, for the name recalled much that he would gladly have forgotten in the novel excitement of the hour. Lucia's love, Edward's parting words, his own reserve so strangely thrown aside, so difficult to resume. What he would have said was checked by the sight of a half-open letter which fell from Jean's dress as she moved away. Mechanically he took it up to return it, and, as he did so, he recognized Sydney's handwriting. Jean snatched it from him, turning pale to the lips as she cried, "Did you read it? What did you see? Tell me, tell me, on your honor!"

"On my honor, I saw nothing but this single sentence, 'By the love I bear you, believe what I say.' No more, as I am a gentleman. I know the hand, I guess the purport of the letter, and as a friend of Sydney, I earnestly desire to help you, if I can. Is this the matter upon which you want advice?"

"Yes."

"Then let me give it?"

"You cannot, without knowing all, and it is so hard to tell!"

"Let me guess it, and spare you the pain of telling. May I?" And Coventry waited eagerly for her reply, for the spell was still upon him.

Holding the letter fast, she beckoned him to follow, and glided before him to a secluded little nook, half boudoir, half conservatory. There she paused, stood an instant as if in doubt, then looked up at him with confiding eyes and said decidedly, "I will do it; for, strange as it may seem, you are the only person to whom I *can* speak. You know Sydney, you have discovered that I am an equal, you have offered your help. I accept it; but oh, do not think me unwomanly! Remember how alone I am, how young, and how much I rely upon your sincerity, your sympathy!"

"Speak freely. I am indeed your friend." And Coventry sat down beside her, forgetful of everything but the soft-eyed girl who confided in him so entirely.

Speaking rapidly, Jean went on, "You know that Sydney loved me, that I refused him and went away. But you do not know that his importunities nearly drove me wild, that he threatened to rob me of my only treasure, my good name, and that, in desperation, I tried to kill myself. Yes, mad, wicked as it was, I did long to end the life which was, at best, a burden, and under his persecution had become a torment. You are shocked, yet what I say is the living truth. Lady Sydney will confirm it, the nurses at the hospital will confess that it was not a fever which brought me there; and here, though the external wound is healed, my heart still aches and burns with the shame and indignation which only a proud woman can feel."

She paused and sat with kindling eyes, glowing cheeks, and both hands pressed to her heaving bosom, as if the old insult roused her spirit anew. Coventry said not a word, for surprise, anger, incredulity, and admiration mingled so confusedly in his mind that he forgot to speak, and Jean went on, "That wild act of mine convinced him of my indomitable dislike. He went away, and I believed that this stormy love of his would be cured by absence. It is not, and I live in daily fear of fresh entreaties, renewed persecution. His mother promised not to betray where I had gone, but he found me out and wrote to me. The letter I asked you to take to Lady Sydney was a reply to his, imploring him to leave me in peace. You failed to deliver it, and I was glad, for I thought silence might quench hope. All in vain; this is a more passionate appeal than ever, and he vows he will never desist from his endeavors till I give another man the right to protect me. I *can* do this—I am sorely tempted to do it, but I rebel against the cruelty. I love my freedom, I have no wish to marry at this man's bidding. What can I do? How can I free myself? Be my friend, and help me!"

Tears streamed down her cheeks, sobs choked her words, and she clasped her hands imploringly as she turned toward the young man in all the abandonment of sorrow, fear, and supplication. Coventry found it hard to meet those eloquent eyes and answer calmly, for he had no experience in such scenes and knew not how to play his part. It is this absurd dress and that romantic nonsense which makes me feel so unlike myself, he thought, quite unconscious of the dangerous power which the dusky room, the midsummer warmth and fragrance, the memory of the "romantic nonsense," and, most of all, the presence of a beautiful, afflicted woman had over him. His usual self-possession deserted him, and he could only echo the words which had made the strongest impression upon him:

"You *can* do this, you are tempted to do it. Is Ned the man who can protect you?"

"No" was the soft reply.

"Who then?"

"Do not ask me. A good and honorable man; one who loves me well, and would devote his life to me; one whom once it would have been happiness to marry, but now—"

There her voice ended in a sigh, and all her fair hair fell down about her face, hiding it in a shining veil.

"Why not now? This is a sure and speedy way of ending your distress. Is it impossible?"

In spite of himself, Gerald leaned nearer, took one of the little hands in his, and pressed it as he spoke, urgently, compassionately, nay, almost tenderly. From behind the veil came a heavy sigh, and the brief answer, "It is impossible."

"Why, Jean?"

She flung her hair back with a sudden gesture, drew away her hand, and answered, almost fiercely, "Because I do not love him! Why do you torment me with such questions? I tell you I am in a sore strait and cannot see my way. Shall I deceive the good man, and secure peace at the price of liberty and truth? Or shall I defy Sydney and lead a life of dread? If he menaced my life, I should not fear; but he menaces that which is dearer than life—my good name. A look, a word can tarnish it; a scornful smile, a significant shrug can do me more harm than any blow;

for I am a woman—friendless, poor, and at the mercy of his tongue. Ah, better to have died, and so have been saved the bitter pain that has come now!"

She sprang up, clasped her hands over her head, and paced despairingly through the little room, not weeping, but wearing an expression more tragical than tears. Still feeling as if he had suddenly stepped into a romance, yet finding a keen pleasure in the part assigned him, Coventry threw himself into it with spirit, and heartily did his best to console the poor girl who needed help so much. Going to her, he said as impetuously as Ned ever did, "Miss Muir—nay, I will say Jean, if that will comfort you—listen, and rest assured that no harm shall touch you if I can ward it off. You are needlessly alarmed. Indignant you may well be, but, upon my life, I think you wrong Sydney. He is violent, I know, but he is too honorable a man to injure you by a light word, an unjust act. He did but threaten, hoping to soften you. Let me see him, or write to him. He is my friend; he will listen to me. Of that I am sure."

"Be sure of nothing. When a man like Sydney loves and is thwarted in his love, nothing can control his headstrong will. Promise me you will not see or write to him. Much as I fear and despise him, I will submit, rather than any harm should befall you—or your brother. You promise me, Mr. Coventry?"

He hesitated. She clung to his arm with unfeigned solicitude in her eager, pleading face, and he could not resist it.

"I promise; but in return you must promise to let me give what help I can; and, Jean, never say again that you are friendless."

"You are so kind! God bless you for it. But I dare not accept your friendship; she will not permit it, and I have no right to mar her peace."

"Who will not permit it?" he demanded hotly.

"Miss Beaufort."

"Hang Miss Beaufort!" exclaimed Coventry, with such energy that Jean broke into a musical laugh, despite her trouble. He joined in it, and, for an instant they stood looking at one another as if the last barrier were down, and they were friends indeed. Jean paused suddenly, with the smile on her lips, the tears still on her cheek, and made a warning gesture. He listened: the sound of feet mingled with calls and laughter proved that they were missed and sought.

"That laugh betrayed us. Stay and meet them. I cannot." And Jean darted out upon the lawn. Coventry followed; for the thought of confronting so many eyes, so many questions, daunted him, and he fled like a coward. The sound of Jean's flying footsteps guided him, and he overtook her just as she paused behind a rose thicket to take breath.

"Fainthearted knight! You should have stayed and covered my retreat. Hark! they are coming! Hide! Hide!" she panted, half in fear, half in merriment, as the gay pursuers rapidly drew nearer.

"Kneel down; the moon is coming out and the glitter of your embroidery will betray you," whispered Jean, as they cowered behind the roses.

"Your arms and hair will betray you. 'Come under my plaiddie,' as the song says." And Coventry tried to make his velvet cloak cover the white shoulders and fair locks.

"We are acting our parts in reality now. How Bella will enjoy the thing when I tell her!" said Jean as the noises died away.

"Do not tell her," whispered Coventry.

"And why not?" she asked, looking up into the face so near her own, with an artless glance.

"Can you not guess why?"

"Ah, you are so proud you cannot bear to be laughed at."

"It is not that. It is because I do not want you to be annoyed by silly tongues; you have enough to pain you without that. I am your friend, now, and I do my best to prove it."

"So kind, so kind! How can I thank you?" murmured Jean. And she involuntarily nestled closer under the cloak that sheltered both.

Neither spoke for a moment, and in the silence the rapid beating of two hearts was heard. To drown the sound, Coventry said softly, "Are you frightened?"

"No, I like it," she answered, as softly, then added abruptly, "But why do we hide? There is nothing to fear. It is late. I must go. You are kneeling on my train. Please rise."

"Why in such haste? This flight and search only adds to the charm of the evening. I'll not get up yet. Will you have a rose, Jean?"

"No, I will not. Let me go, Mr. Coventry, I insist. There has been enough of this folly. You forget yourself."

She spoke imperiously, flung off the cloak, and put him from her. He rose at once, saying, like one waking suddenly from a pleasant dream, "I do indeed forget myself."

Here the sound of voices broke on them, nearer than before. Pointing to a covered walk that led to the house, he said, in his usually cool, calm tone, "Go in that way; I will cover your retreat." And turning, he went to meet the merry hunters.

Half an hour later, when the party broke up, Miss Muir joined them in her usual quiet dress, looking paler, meeker, and sadder than usual. Coventry saw this, though he neither looked at her nor addressed her. Lucia saw it also, and was glad that the dangerous girl had fallen back into her proper place again, for she had suffered much that night. She appropriated her cousin's arm as they went through the park, but he was in one of his taciturn moods, and all her attempts at conversation were in vain. Miss Muir walked alone, singing softly to herself as she followed in the dusk. Was Gerald so silent because he listened to that fitful song?

Lucia thought so, and felt her dislike rapidly deepening to hatred.

When the young friends were gone, and the family were exchanging good-nights among themselves, Jean was surprised by Coventry's offering his hand, for he had never done it before, and whispering, as he held it, though Lucia watched him all the while, "I have not given my advice, yet."

"Thanks, I no longer need it. I have decided for myself."

"May I ask how?"

"To brave my enemy."

"Good! But what decided you so suddenly?"

"The finding of a friend." And with a grateful glance she was gone.

CHAPTER VI

ON THE WATCH

"If you please, Mr. Coventry, did you get the letter last night?" were the first words that greeted the "young master" as he left his room next morning.

"What letter, Dean? I don't remember any," he answered, pausing, for something in the maid's manner struck him as peculiar.

"It came just as you left for the Hall, sir. Benson ran after you with it, as it was marked 'Haste.' Didn't you get it, sir?" asked the woman, anxiously.

"Yes, but upon my life, I forgot all about it till this minute. It's in my other coat, I suppose, if I've not lost it. That absurd masquerading put everything else out of my head." And speaking more to himself than to the maid, Coventry turned back to look for the missing letter.

Dean remained where she was, apparently busy about the arrangement of the curtains at the hall window, but furtively watching meanwhile with a most unwonted air of curiosity.

"Not there, I thought so!" she muttered, as Coventry impatiently thrust his hand into one pocket after another. But as she spoke, an expression of amazement appeared in her face, for suddenly the letter was discovered.

"I'd have sworn it wasn't there! I don't understand it, but she's a deep one, or I'm much deceived." And Dean shook her head like one perplexed, but not convinced.

Coventry uttered an exclamation of satisfaction on glancing at the address and, standing where he was, tore open the letter.

> *Dear C:*
>
> *I'm off to Baden. Come and join me, then you'll be out of harm's way; for if you fall in love with J.M. (and you can't escape if you stay where she is), you will incur the trifling inconvenience of having your brains blown out by*
>
> *Yours truly, F.R. Sydney*

"The man is mad!" ejaculated Coventry, staring at the letter while an angry flush rose to his face. "What the deuce does he mean by writing to me in that style? Join him — not I! And as for the threat, I laugh at it. Poor Jean! This headstrong fool seems bent on tormenting her. Well, Dean, what are you waiting for?" he demand-ed, as if suddenly conscious of her presence.

"Nothing, sir; I only stopped to see if you found the letter. Beg pardon, sir."

And she was moving on when Coventry asked, with a suspicious look, "What made you think it was lost? You seem to take an uncommon interest in my affairs today."

"Oh dear, no, sir. I felt a bit anxious, Benson is so forgetful, and it was me who sent him after you, for I happened to see you go out, so I felt responsible. Being marked that way, I thought it might be important so I asked about it."

"Very well, you can go, Dean. It's all right, you see."

"I'm not so sure of that," muttered the woman, as she curtsied respectfully and went away, looking as if the letter had *not* been found.

Dean was Miss Beaufort's maid, a grave, middle-aged woman with keen eyes and a somewhat grim air. Having been long in the family, she enjoyed all the privileges of a faithful and favorite servant. She loved her young mistress with an almost jealous affection. She watched over her with the vigilant care of a mother and resented any attempt at interference on the part of others. At first she had pitied and liked Jean Muir, then distrusted her, and now heartily hated her, as the cause of the increased indifference of Coventry toward his cousin. Dean knew the depth of Lucia's love, and though no man, in her eyes, was worthy of her mistress, still, having honored him with her regard, Dean felt bound to like him, and the late change in his manner disturbed the maid almost as much as it did the mistress. She watched Jean narrowly, causing that amiable creature much amusement but little annoyance, as yet, for Dean's slow English wit was no match for the subtle mind of the governess. On the preceding night, Dean had been sent up to the Hall with costumes and had there seen something which much disturbed her. She be-gan to speak of it while undressing her mistress, but Lucia, being in an unhappy mood, had so sternly ordered her not to gossip that the tale remained untold, and she was forced to bide her tune.

Now I'll see how *she* looks after it; though there's not much to be got out of *her* face, the deceitful hussy, thought Dean, marching down the corridor and knitting her black brows as she went.

"Good morning, Mrs. Dean. I hope you are none the worse for last night's frol-ic. You had the work and we the play," said a blithe voice behind her; and turning sharply, she confronted Miss Muir. Fresh and smiling, the governess nodded with an air of cordiality which would have been irresistible with anyone but Dean.

"I'm quite well, thank you, miss," she returned coldly, as her keen eye fas-tened on the girl as if to watch the effect of her words. "I had a good rest when the young ladies and gentlemen were at supper, for while the maids cleared up, I sat in the 'little anteroom.'"

"Yes, I saw you, and feared you'd take cold. Very glad you didn't. How is Miss

Beaufort? She seemed rather poorly last night" was the tranquil reply, as Jean settled the little frills about her delicate wrists. The cool question was a return shot for Dean's hint that she had been where she could oversee the interview between Coventry and Miss Muir.

"She is a bit tired, as any *lady* would be after such an evening. People who are *used* to *play-acting* wouldn't mind it, perhaps, but Miss Beaufort don't enjoy *romps* as much as *some* do."

The emphasis upon certain words made Dean's speech as impertinent as she desired. But Jean only laughed, and as Coventry's step was heard behind them, she ran downstairs, saying blandly, but with a wicked look, "I won't stop to thank you now, lest Mr. Coventry should bid me good-morning, and so increase Miss Beaufort's indisposition."

Dean's eyes flashed as she looked after the girl with a wrathful face, and went her way, saying grimly, "I'll bide my time, but I'll get the better of her yet."

Fancying himself quite removed from "last night's absurdity," yet curious to see how Jean would meet him, Coventry lounged into the breakfast room with his usual air of listless indifference. A languid nod and murmur was all the reply he vouchsafed to the greetings of cousin, sister, and governess as he sat down and took up his paper.

"Have you had a letter from Ned?" asked Bella, looking at the note which her brother still held.

"No" was the brief answer.

"Who then? You look as if you had received bad news."

There was no reply, and, peeping over his arm, Bella caught sight of the seal and exclaimed, in a disappointed tone, "It is the Sydney crest. I don't care about the note now. Men's letters to each other are not interesting."

Miss Muir had been quietly feeding one of Edward's dogs, but at the name she looked up and met Coventry's eyes, coloring so distressfully that he pitied her. Why he should take the trouble to cover her confusion, he did not stop to ask himself, but seeing the curl of Lucia's lip, he suddenly addressed her with an air of displeasure, "Do you know that Dean is getting impertinent? She presumes too much on her age and your indulgence, and forgets her place."

"What has she done?" asked Lucia coldly.

"She troubles herself about my affairs and takes it upon herself to keep Benson in order."

Here Coventry told about the letter and the woman's evident curiosity.

"Poor Dean, she gets no thanks for reminding you of what you had forgotten. Next time she will leave your letters to their fate, and perhaps it will be as well, if they have such a bad effect upon your temper, Gerald."

Lucia spoke calmly, but there was an angry color in her cheek as she rose and left the room. Coventry looked much annoyed, for on Jean's face he detected a faint smile, half pitiful, half satirical, which disturbed him more than his cousin's insinuation. Bella broke the awkward silence by saying, with a sigh, "Poor Ned! I do so long to hear again from him. I thought a letter had come for some of us. Dean said she saw one bearing his writing on the hall table yesterday."

"She seems to have a mania for inspecting letters. I won't allow it. Who was the letter for, Bella?" said Coventry, putting down his paper.

"She wouldn't or couldn't tell, but looked very cross and told me to ask you."

"Very odd! I've had none," began Coventry.

"But I had one several days ago. Will you please read it, and my reply?" And as she spoke, Jean laid two letters before him.

"Certainly not. It would be dishonorable to read what Ned intended for no eyes but your own. You are too scrupulous in one way, and not enough so in another, Miss Muir." And Coventry offered both the letters with an air of grave decision, which could not conceal the interest and surprise he felt.

"You are right. Mr. Edward's note *should* be kept sacred, for in it the poor boy has laid bare his heart to me. But mine I beg you will read, that you may see how well I try to keep my word to you. Oblige me in this, Mr. Coventry; I have a right to ask it of you."

So urgently she spoke, so wistfully she looked, that he could not refuse and, going to the window, read the letter. It was evidently an answer to a passionate appeal from the young lover, and was written with consummate skill. As he read, Gerald could not help thinking, If this girl writes in this way to a man whom she does *not* love, with what a world of power and passion would she write to one whom she *did* love. And this thought kept returning to him as his eye went over line after line of wise argument, gentle reproof, good counsel, and friendly regard. Here and there a word, a phrase, betrayed what she had already confessed, and Coventry forgot to return the letter, as he stood wondering who was the man whom Jean loved.

The sound of Bella's voice recalled him, for she was saying, half kindly, half petulantly, "Don't look so sad, Jean. Ned will outlive it, I dare say. You remember you said once men never died of love, though women might. In his one note to me, he spoke so beautifully of you, and begged me to be kind to you for his sake, that I try to be with all my heart, though if it was anyone but you, I really think I should hate them for making my dear boy so unhappy."

"You are too kind, Bella, and I often think I'll go away to relieve you of my presence; but unwise and dangerous as it is to stay, I haven't the courage to go. I've been so happy here." And as she spoke, Jean's head dropped lower over the dog as it nestled to her affectionately.

Before Bella could utter half the loving words that sprang to her lips, Coventry came to them with all languor gone from face and mien, and laying Jean's letter before her, he said, with an undertone of deep feeling in his usually emotionless voice, "A right womanly and eloquent letter, but I fear it will only increase the fire it was meant to quench. I pity my brother more than ever now."

"Shall I send it?" asked Jean, looking straight up at him, like one who had entire reliance on his judgment.

"Yes, I have not the heart to rob him of such a sweet sermon upon self-sacrifice. Shall I post it for you?"

"Thank you; in a moment." And with a grateful look, Jean dropped her eyes. Producing her little purse, she selected a penny, folded it in a bit of paper, and then offered both letter and coin to Coventry, with such a pretty air of business, that he could not control a laugh.

"So you won't be indebted to me for a penny? What a proud woman you are, Miss Muir."

"I am; it's a family failing." And she gave him a significant glance, which recalled to him the memory of who she was. He understood her feeling, and liked her the better for it, knowing that he would have done the same had he been in her place. It was a little thing, but if done for effect, it answered admirably, for it showed a quick insight into his character on her part, and betrayed to him the existence of a pride in which he sympathized heartily. He stood by Jean a moment, watching her as she burnt Edward's letter in the blaze of the spirit lamp under the urn.

"Why do you do that?" he asked involuntarily.

"Because it is my duty to forget" was all her answer.

"Can you always forget when it becomes a duty?"

"I wish I could! I wish I could!"

She spoke passionately, as if the words broke from her against her will, and, rising hastily, she went into the garden, as if afraid to stay.

"Poor, dear Jean is very unhappy about something, but I can't discover what it is. Last night I found her crying over a rose, and now she runs away, looking as if her heart was broken. I'm glad I've got no lessons."

"What kind of a rose?" asked Coventry from behind his paper as Bella paused.

"A lovely white one. It must have come from the Hall; we have none like it. I wonder if Jean was ever going to be married, and lost her lover, and felt sad because the flower reminded her of bridal roses."

Coventry made no reply, but felt himself change countenance as he recalled the little scene behind the rose hedge, where he gave Jean the flower which she had refused yet taken. Presently, to Bella's surprise, he flung down the paper, tore Sydney's note to atoms, and rang for his horse with an energy which amazed her.

"Why, Gerald, what has come over you? One would think Ned's restless spirit had suddenly taken possession of you. What are you going to do?"

"I'm going to work" was the unexpected answer, as Coventry turned toward her with an expression so rarely seen on his fine face.

"What has waked you up all at once?" asked Bella, looking more and more amazed.

"You did," he said, drawing her toward him.

"I! When? How?"

"Do you remember saying once that energy was better than beauty in a man, and that no one could respect an idler?"

"I never said anything half so sensible as that. Jean said something like it once, I believe, but I forgot. Are you tired of doing nothing, at last, Gerald?"

"Yes, I neglected my duty to Ned, till he got into trouble, and now I reproach myself for it. It's not too late to do other neglected tasks, so I'm going at them with a will. Don't say anything about it to anyone, and don't laugh at me, for I'm in earnest, Bell."

"I know you are, and I admire and love you for it, my dear old boy," cried Bella enthusiastically, as she threw her arms about his neck and kissed him heartily. "What will you do first?" she asked, as he stood thoughtfully smoothing the bright head that leaned upon his shoulder, with that new expression still clear and steady in his face.

"I'm going to ride over the whole estate, and attend to things as a master should; not leave it all to Bent, of whom I've heard many complaints, but have been too idle to inquire about them. I shall consult Uncle, and endeavor to be all that my father was in his time. Is that a worthy ambition, dear?"

"Oh, Gerald, let me tell Mamma. It will make her so happy. You are her idol, and to hear you say these things, to see you look so like dear Papa, would do more for her spirits than all the doctors in England."

"Wait till I prove what my resolution is worth. When I have really done something, then I'll surprise Mamma with a sample of my work."

"Of course you'll tell Lucia?"

"Not on any account. It is a little secret between us, so keep it till I give you leave to tell it."

"But Jean will see it at once; she knows everything that happens, she is so quick and wise. Do you mind her knowing?"

"I don't see that I can help it if she is so wonderfully gifted. Let her see what she can, I don't mind her. Now I'm off." And with a kiss to his sister, a sudden smile on his face, Coventry sprang upon his horse and rode away at a pace which caused the groom to stare after him in blank amazement.

Nothing more was seen of him till dinnertime, when he came in so exhilarated by his brisk ride and busy morning that he found some difficulty in assuming his customary manner, and more than once astonished the family by talking animatedly on various subjects which till now had always seemed utterly uninteresting to him. Lucia was amazed, his mother delighted, and Bella could hardly control her desire to explain the mystery; but Jean took it very calmly and regarded him with the air of one who said, "I understand, but you will soon tire of it." This nettled him more than he would confess, and he exerted himself to silently contradict that prophecy.

"Have you answered Mr. Sydney's letter?" asked Bella, when they were all scattered about the drawing room after dinner.

"No," answered her brother, who was pacing up and down with restless steps, instead of lounging near his beautiful cousin.

"I ask because I remembered that Ned sent a message for him in my last note, as he thought you would know Sydney's address. Here it is, something about a horse. Please put it in when you write," and Bella laid the note on the writing table nearby.

"I'll send it at once and have done with it," muttered Coventry and, seating himself, he dashed off a few lines, sealed and sent the letter, and then resumed his march, eyeing the three young ladies with three different expressions, as he passed and repassed. Lucia sat apart, feigning to be intent upon a book, and her handsome face looked almost stern in its haughty composure, for though her heart ached, she was too proud to own it. Bella now lay on the sofa, half asleep, a rosy little creature, as unconsciously pretty as a child. Miss Muir sat in the recess of a deep window, in a low lounging chair, working at an embroidery frame with a graceful industry pleasant to see. Of late she had worn colors, for Bella had been generous in gifts, and the pale blue muslin which flowed in soft waves about her was very becoming to her fair skin and golden hair. The close braids were gone, and loose curls dropped here and there from the heavy coil wound around her well-shaped head. The tip of one dainty foot was visible, and a petulant little gesture which now and then shook back the falling sleeve gave glimpses of a round white arm. Ned's great hound lay nearby, the sunshine flickered on her through the leaves, and as she sat smiling to herself, while the dexterous hands shaped leaf and flower, she made a charming picture of all that is most womanly and winning; a picture which few men's eyes would not have liked to rest upon.

Another chair stood near her, and as Coventry went up and down, a strong desire to take it possessed him. He was tired of his thoughts and wished to be amused by watching the changes of the girl's expressive face, listening to the varying tones of her voice, and trying to discover the spell which so strongly attracted him in spite of himself. More than once he swerved from his course to gratify his whim, but Lucia's presence always restrained him, and with a word to the dog, or a glance from the window, as pretext for a pause, he resumed his walk again. Something in his cousin's face reproached him, but her manner of late was so repellent that he felt no desire to resume their former familiarity, and, wishing to show that he did not consider himself bound, he kept aloof. It was a quiet test of the power of each woman over this man; they instinctively felt it, and both tried to conquer. Lucia spoke several times, and tried to speak frankly and affably; but her manner was constrained, and Coventry, having answered politely, relapsed into silence. Jean said nothing, but silently appealed to eye and ear by the pretty picture she made of herself, the snatches of song she softly sang, as if forgetting that she was not alone, and a shy glance now and then, half wistful, half merry, which was more alluring than graceful figure or sweet voice. When she had tormented Lucia and tempted Coventry long enough, she quietly asserted her supremacy in a way which astonished her rival, who knew nothing of the secret of her birth, which knowledge did much to attract and charm the young man. Letting a ball of silk escape from her lap, she watched it roll toward the promenader, who caught and returned it with an alacrity which added grace to the trifling service. As she took it, she said, in the frank way that never failed to win him, "I think you must be tired; but if exercise is necessary, employ your energies to some purpose and put your mother's basket of silks in order. They are in a tangle, and it will please her to know that you did it, as your brother used to do."

"Hercules at the distaff," said Coventry gaily, and down he sat in the long-desired seat. Jean put the basket on his knee, and as he surveyed it, as if daunted at his task, she leaned back, and indulged in a musical little peal of laughter charming to hear. Lucia sat dumb with surprise, to see her proud, indolent cousin obeying the commands of a governess, and looking as if he heartily enjoyed it. In ten minutes she was as entirely forgotten as if she had been miles away; for Jean seemed in her wittiest, gayest mood, and as she now treated the "young master" like an equal, there was none of the former meek timidity. Yet often her eyes fell, her color changed, and the piquant sallies faltered on her tongue, as Coventry involuntarily looked deep into the fine eyes which had once shone on him so tenderly in that mimic tragedy. He could not forget it, and though neither alluded to it, the memory of the previous evening seemed to haunt both and lend a secret charm to the present moment. Lucia bore this as long as she could, and then left the room with the air of an insulted princess; but Coventry did not, and Jean feigned not to see her go. Bella was fast asleep, and before he knew how it came to pass, the young man was listening to the story of his companion's life. A sad tale, told with wonderful skill, for soon he was absorbed in it. The basket slid unobserved from his knee, the dog was pushed away, and, leaning forward, he listened eagerly as the girl's low voice recounted all the hardships, loneliness, and grief of her short life. In the midst of a touching episode she started, stopped, and looked straight before her, with an intent expression which changed to one of intense contempt, and her eye turned to Coventry's, as she said, pointing to the window behind him, "We are watched."

"By whom?" he demanded, starting up angrily.

"Hush, say nothing, let it pass. I am used to it."

"But *I* am not, and I'll not submit to it. Who was it, Jean?" he answered hotly.

She smiled significantly at a knot of rose-colored ribbon, which a little gust was blowing toward them along the terrace. A black frown darkened the young man's face as he sprang out of the long window and went rapidly out of sight, scrutinizing each green nook as he passed. Jean laughed quietly as she watched him, and said softly to herself, with her eyes on the fluttering ribbon, "That was a fortunate accident, and a happy inspiration. Yes, my dear Mrs. Dean, you will find that playing the spy will only get your mistress as well as yourself into trouble. You would not be warned, and you must take the consequences, reluctant as I am to injure a worthy creature like yourself."

Soon Coventry was heard returning. Jean listened with suspended breath to catch his first words, for he was not alone.

"Since you insist that it was you and not your mistress, I let it pass, although I still have my suspicions. Tell Miss Beaufort I desire to see her for a few moments in the library. Now go, Dean, and be careful for the future, if you wish to stay in my house."

The maid retired, and the young man came in looking both ireful and stern.

"I wish I had said nothing, but I was startled, and spoke involuntarily. Now you are angry, and I have made fresh trouble for poor Miss Lucia. Forgive me as I forgive her, and let it pass. I have learned to bear this surveillance, and pity her causeless jealousy," said Jean, with a self-reproachful air.

"I will forgive the dishonorable act, but I cannot forget it, and I intend to put a stop to it. I am not betrothed to my cousin, as I told you once, but you, like all the rest, seem bent on believing that I am. Hitherto I have cared too little about the matter to settle it, but now I shall prove beyond all doubt that I am free."

As he uttered the last word, Coventry cast on Jean a look that affected her strangely. She grew pale, her work dropped on her lap, and her eyes rose to his, with an eager, questioning expression, which slowly changed to one of mingled pain and pity, as she turned her face away, murmuring in a tone of tender sorrow, "Poor Lucia, who will comfort her?"

For a moment Coventry stood silent, as if weighing some fateful purpose in his mind. As Jean's rapt sigh of compassion reached his ear, he had echoed it within himself, and half repented of his resolution; then his eye rested on the girl before him looking so lonely in her sweet sympathy for another that his heart yearned toward her. Sudden fire shot into his eye, sudden warmth replaced the cold sternness of his face, and his steady voice faltered suddenly, as he said, very low, yet very earnestly, "Jean, I have tried to love her, but I cannot. Ought I to deceive her, and make myself miserable to please my family?"

"She is beautiful and good, and loves you tenderly; is there no hope for her?" asked Jean, still pale, but very quiet, though she held one hand against her heart, as if to still or hide its rapid beating.

"None," answered Coventry.

"But can you not learn to love her? Your will is strong, and most men would not find it a hard task."

"I cannot, for something stronger than my own will controls me."

"What is that?" And Jean's dark eyes were fixed upon him, full of innocent wonder.

His fell, and he said hastily, "I dare not tell you yet."

"Pardon! I should not have asked. Do not consult me in this matter; I am not the person to advise you. I can only say that it seems to me as if any man with an empty heart would be glad to have so beautiful a woman as your cousin."

"My heart is not empty," began Coventry, drawing a step nearer, and speaking in a passionate voice. "Jean, I *must* speak; hear me. I cannot love my cousin, because I love you."

"Stop!" And Jean sprang up with a commanding gesture. "I will not hear you while any promise binds you to another. Remember your mother's wishes, Lucia's hopes, Edward's last words, your own pride, my humble lot. You forget yourself, Mr. Coventry. Think well before you speak, weigh the cost of this act, and recollect who I am before you insult me by any transient passion, any false vows."

"I have thought, I do weigh the cost, and I swear that I desire to woo you as humbly, honestly as I would any lady in the land. You speak of my pride. Do I stoop in loving my equal in rank? You speak of your lowly lot, but poverty is no disgrace, and the courage with which you bear it makes it beautiful. I should have broken with Lucia before I spoke, but I could not control myself. My mother loves you, and will be happy in my happiness. Edward must forgive me, for I have tried to do my best, but love is irresistible. Tell me, Jean, is there any hope for me?"

He had seized her hand and was speaking impetuously, with ardent face and tender tone, but no answer came, for as Jean turned her eloquent countenance toward him, full of maiden shame and timid love, Dean's prim figure appeared at the door, and her harsh voice broke the momentary silence, saying, sternly, "Miss Beaufort is waiting for you, sir."

"Go, go at once, and be kind, for my sake, Gerald," whispered Jean, for he stood as if deaf and blind to everything but her voice, her face.

As she drew his head down to whisper, her cheek touched his, and regardless of Dean, he kissed it, passionately, whispering back, "My little Jean! For your sake I can be anything."

"Miss Beaufort is waiting. Shall I say you will come, sir?" demanded Dean, pale and grim with indignation.

"Yes, yes, I'll come. Wait for me in the garden, Jean." And Coventry hurried away, in no mood for the interview but anxious to have it over.

As the door closed behind him, Dean walked up to Miss Muir, trembling with anger, and laying a heavy hand on her arm, she said below her breath, "I've been expecting this, you artful creature. I saw your game and did my best to spoil it, but you are too quick for me. You think you've got him. There you are mistaken; for as sure as my name is Hester Dean, I'll prevent it, or Sir John shall."

"Take your hand away and treat me with proper respect, or you will be dismissed from this house. Do you know who I am?" And Jean drew herself up with a haughty air, which impressed the woman more deeply than her words. "I am the daughter of Lady Howard and, if I choose it, can be the wife of Mr. Coventry."

Dean drew back amazed, yet not convinced. Being a well-trained servant, as well as a prudent woman, she feared to overstep the bounds of respect, to go too far, and get her mistress as well as herself into trouble. So, though she still doubted Jean, and hated her more than ever, she controlled herself. Dropping a curtsy, she assumed her usual air of deference, and said, meekly, "I beg pardon, miss. If I'd known, I should have conducted myself differently, of course, but ordinary governesses make so much mischief in a house, one can't help mistrusting them. I don't wish to meddle or be overbold, but being fond of my dear young lady, I naturally take her part, and must say that Mr. Coventry has not acted like a gentleman."

"Think what you please, Dean, but I advise you to say as little as possible if you wish to remain. I have not accepted Mr. Coventry yet, and if he chooses to set aside the engagement his family made for him, I think he has a right to do so. Miss Beaufort would hardly care to marry him against his will, because he pities her for her unhappy love," and with a tranquil smile, Miss Muir walked away.

CHAPTER VII

THE LAST CHANCE

"She will tell Sir John, will she? Then I must be before her, and hasten events. It will be as well to have all sure before there can be any danger. My poor Dean, you are no match for me, but you may prove annoying, nevertheless."

These thoughts passed through Miss Muir's mind as she went down the hall, pausing an instant at the library door, for the murmur of voices was heard. She caught no word, and had only time for an instant's pause as Dean's heavy step followed her. Turning, Jean drew a chair before the door, and, beckoning to the woman, she said, smiling still, "Sit here and play watchdog. I am going to Miss Bella, so you can nod if you will."

"Thank you, miss. I will wait for my young lady. She may need me when this hard time is over." And Dean seated herself with a resolute face.

Jean laughed and went on; but her eyes gleamed with sudden malice, and she glanced over her shoulder with an expression which boded ill for the faithful old servant.

"I've got a letter from Ned, and here is a tiny note for you," cried Bella as Jean entered the boudoir. "Mine is a very odd, hasty letter, with no news in it, but his meeting with Sydney. I hope yours is better, or it won't be very satisfactory."

As Sydney's name passed Bella's lips, all the color died out of Miss Muir's face, and the note shook with the tremor of her hand. Her very lips were white, but she said calmly, "Thank you. As you are busy, I'll go and read my letter on the lawn." And before Bella could speak, she was gone.

Hurrying to a quiet nook, Jean tore open the note and read the few blotted lines it contained.

I have seen Sydney; he has told me all; and, hard as I found it to believe, it was impossible to doubt, for he has discovered proofs which cannot be denied. I make no reproaches, shall demand no confession or atonement, for I cannot forget that I once loved you. I give you three days to find another home, before I return to tell the family who you are. Go at once, I beseech you, and spare me the pain of seeing your disgrace.

Slowly, steadily she read it twice over, then sat motionless, knitting her brows in deep thought. Presently she drew a long breath, tore up the note, and rising, went slowly toward the Hall, saying to herself, "Three days, only three days! Can it be accomplished in so short a time? It shall be, if wit and will can do it, for it is my last chance. If this fails, I'll not go back to my old life, but end all at once."

Setting her teeth and clenching her hands, as if some memory stung her, she went on through the twilight, to find Sir John waiting to give her a hearty welcome.

"You look tired, my dear. Never mind the reading tonight; rest yourself, and let the book go," he said kindly, observing her worn look.

"Thank you, sir. I am tired, but I'd rather read, else the book will not be finished before I go."

"Go, child! Where are you going?" demanded Sir John, looking anxiously at her as she sat down.

"I will tell you by-and-by, sir." And opening the book, Jean read for a little while.

But the usual charm was gone; there was no spirit in the voice of the reader, no interest in the face of the listener, and soon he said, abruptly, "My dear, pray stop! I cannot listen with a divided mind. What troubles you? Tell your friend, and let him comfort you."

As if the kind words overcame her, Jean dropped the book, covered up her face, and wept so bitterly that Sir John was much alarmed; for such a demonstration was doubly touching in one who usually was all gaiety and smiles. As he tried to soothe her, his words grew tender, his solicitude full of a more than paternal anxiety, and his kind heart overflowed with pity and affection for the weeping girl. As she grew calmer, he urged her to be frank, promising to help and counsel her, whatever the affliction or fault might be.

"Ah, you are too kind, too generous! How can I go away and leave my one friend?" sighed Jean, wiping the tears away and looking up at him with grateful eyes.

"Then you do care a little for the old man?" said Sir John with an eager look, an involuntary pressure of the hand he held.

Jean turned her face away, and answered, very low, "No one ever was so kind to me as you have been. Can I help caring for you more than I can express?"

Sir John was a little deaf at times, but he heard that, and looked well pleased. He had been rather thoughtful of late, had dressed with unusual care, been particularly gallant and gay when the young ladies visited him, and more than once, when Jean paused in the reading to ask a question, he had been forced to confess that he had not been listening; though, as she well knew, his eyes had been fixed upon her. Since the discovery of her birth, his manner had been peculiarly benignant, and many little acts had proved his interest and goodwill. Now, when Jean spoke of going, a panic seized him, and desolation seemed about to fall upon the old Hall. Something in her unusual agitation struck him as peculiar and excited his curiosity. Never had she seemed so interesting as now, when she sat beside him with tearful eyes, and some soft trouble in her heart which she dared not confess.

"Tell me everything, child, and let your friend help you if he can." Formerly he said "father" or "the old man," but lately he always spoke of himself as her "friend."

"I will tell you, for I have no one else to turn to. I must go away because Mr. Coventry has been weak enough to love me."

"What, Gerald?" cried Sir John, amazed.

"Yes; today he told me this, and left me to break with Lucia; so I ran to you to help me prevent him from disappointing his mother's hopes and plans."

Sir John had started up and paced down the room, but as Jean paused he turned toward her, saying, with an altered face, "Then you do not love him? Is it possible?"

"No, I do not love him," she answered promptly.

"Yet he is all that women usually find attractive. How is it that you have escaped, Jean?"

"I love someone else" was the scarcely audible reply.

Sir John resumed his seat with the air of a man bent on getting at a mystery, if possible.

"It will be unjust to let you suffer for the folly of these boys, my little girl. Ned is gone, and I was sure that Gerald was safe; but now that his turn has come, I am perplexed, for he cannot be sent away."

"No, it is I who must go; but it seems so hard to leave this safe and happy home, and wander away into the wide, cold world again. You have all been too kind to me, and now separation breaks my heart."

A sob ended the speech, and Jean's head went down upon her hands again. Sir John looked at her a moment, and his fine old face was full of genuine emotion, as he said slowly, "Jean, will you stay and be a daughter to the solitary old man?"

"No, sir" was the unexpected answer.

"And why not?" asked Sir John, looking surprised, but rather pleased than angry.

"Because I could not be a daughter to you; and even if I could, it would not be wise, for the gossips would say you were not old enough to be the adopted father of a girl like me. Sir John, young as I am, I know much of the world, and am sure that this kind plan is impractical; but I thank you from the bottom of my heart."

"Where will you go, Jean?" asked Sir John, after a pause.

"To London, and try to find another situation where I can do no harm."

"Will it be difficult to find another home?"

"Yes. I cannot ask Mrs. Coventry to recommend me, when I have innocently brought so much trouble into her family; and Lady Sydney is gone, so I have no friend."

"Except John Coventry. I will arrange all that. When will you go, Jean?"

"Tomorrow."

"So soon!" And the old man's voice betrayed the trouble he was trying to conceal.

Jean had grown very calm, but it was the calmness of desperation. She had hoped that the first tears would produce the avowal for which she waited. It had not, and she began to fear that her last chance was slipping from her. Did the old man love her? If so, why did he not speak? Eager to profit by each moment, she was on the alert for any hopeful hint, any propitious word, look, or act, and every nerve was strung to the utmost.

"Jean, may I ask one question?" said Sir John.

"Anything of me, sir."

"This man whom you love—can he not help you?"

"He could if he knew, but he must not."

"If he knew what? Your present trouble?"

"No. My love."

"He does not know this, then?"

"No, thank heaven! And he never will."

"Why not?"

"Because I am too proud to own it."

"He loves you, my child?"

"I do not know—I dare not hope it," murmured Jean.

"Can I not help you here? Believe me, I desire to see you safe and happy. Is there nothing I can do?"

"Nothing, nothing."

"May I know the name?"

"No! No! Let me go; I cannot bear this questioning!" And Jean's distressful face warned him to ask no more.

"Forgive me, and let me do what I may. Rest here quietly. I'll write a letter to a good friend of mine, who will find you a home, if you leave us."

As Sir John passed into his inner study, Jean watched him with despairing eyes and wrung her hands, saying to herself, Has all my skill deserted me when I need it most? How can I make him understand, yet not overstep the bounds of maiden modesty? He is so blind, so timid, or so dull he will not see, and time is going fast. What shall I do to open his eyes?

Her own eyes roved about the room, seeking for some aid from inanimate things, and soon she found it. Close behind the couch where she sat hung a fine miniature of Sir John. At first her eye rested on it as she contrasted its placid comeliness with the unusual pallor and disquiet of the living face seen through the open door, as the old man sat at his desk trying to write and casting covert glances at the girlish figure he had left behind him. Affecting unconsciousness of this, Jean gazed on as if forgetful of everything but the picture, and suddenly, as if obeying an irresistible impulse, she took it down, looked long and fondly at it, then, shaking her curls about her face, as if to hide the act, pressed it to her lips and seemed to weep over it in an uncontrollable paroxysm of tender grief. A sound startled her, and like a guilty thing, she turned to replace the picture; but it dropped from her hand as she uttered a faint cry and hid her face, for Sir John stood before her, with an expression which she could not mistake.

"Jean, why did you do that?" he asked, in an eager, agitated voice.

No answer, as the girl sank lower, like one overwhelmed with shame. Laying his hand on the bent head, and bending his own, he whispered, "Tell me, is the name John Coventry?"

Still no answer, but a stifled sound betrayed that his words had gone home.

"Jean, shall I go back and write the letter, or may I stay and tell you that the old man loves you better than a daughter?"

She did not speak, but a little hand stole out from under the falling hair, as if to keep him. With a broken exclamation he seized it, drew her up into his arms, and laid his gray head on her fair one, too happy for words. For a moment Jean Muir enjoyed her success; then, fearing lest some sudden mishap should destroy it, she hastened to make all secure. Looking up with well-feigned timidity and half-confessed affection, she said softly, "Forgive me that I could not hide this better. I meant to go away and never tell it, but you were so kind it made the parting doubly hard. Why did you ask such dangerous questions? Why did you look, when you should have been writing my dismissal?"

"How could I dream that you loved me, Jean, when you refused the only offer I dared make? Could I be presumptuous enough to fancy you would reject young lovers for an old man like me?" asked Sir John, caressing her.

"You are not old, to me, but everything I love and honor!" interrupted Jean, with a touch of genuine remorse, as this generous, honorable gentleman gave her both heart and home, unconscious of deceit. "It is I who am presumptuous, to dare to love one so far above me. But I did not know how dear you were to me till I felt that I must go. I ought not to accept this happiness. I am not worthy of it; and you will regret your kindness when the world blames you for giving a home to one so poor, and plain, and humble as I."

"Hush, my darling. I care nothing for the idle gossip of the world. If you are happy here, let tongues wag as they will. I shall be too busy enjoying the sunshine of your presence to heed anything that goes on about me. But, Jean, you are sure you love me? It seems incredible that I should win the heart that has been so cold to younger, better men than I."

"Dear Sir John, be sure of this, I love you truly. I will do my best to be a good wife to you, and prove that, in spite of my many faults, I possess the virtue of gratitude."

If he had known the strait she was in, he would have understood the cause of the sudden fervor of her words, the intense thankfulness that shone in her face, the real humility that made her stoop and kiss the generous hand that gave so much. For a few moments she enjoyed and let him enjoy the happy present, undisturbed. But the anxiety which devoured her, the danger which menaced her, soon recalled her, and forced her to wring yet more from the unsuspicious heart she had conquered.

"No need of letters now," said Sir John, as they sat side by side, with the summer moonlight glorifying all the room. "You have found a home for life; may it prove a happy one."

"It is not mine yet, and I have a strange foreboding that it never will be," she answered sadly.

"Why, my child?"

"Because I have an enemy who will try to destroy my peace, to poison your mind against me, and to drive me out from my paradise, to suffer again all I have suffered this last year."

"You mean that mad Sydney of whom you told me?"

"Yes. As soon as he hears of this good fortune to poor little Jean, he will hasten to mar it. He is my fate; I cannot escape him, and wherever he goes my friends desert me; for he has the power and uses it for my destruction. Let me go away and hide before he comes, for, having shared your confidence, it will break my heart to see you distrust and turn from me, instead of loving and protecting."

"My poor child, you are superstitious. Be easy. No one can harm you now, no one would dare attempt it. And as for my deserting you, that will soon be out of my power, if I have my way."

"How, dear Sir John?" asked Jean, with a flutter of intense relief at her heart, for the way seemed smoothing before her.

"I will make you my wife at once, if I may. This will free you from Gerald's love, protect you from Sydney's persecution, give you a safe home, and me the right to cherish and defend with heart and hand. Shall it be so, my child?"

"Yes; but oh, remember that I have no friend but you! Promise me to be faithful to the last—to believe in me, to trust me, protect and love me, in spite of all misfortunes, faults, and follies. I will be true as steel to you, and make your life as happy as it deserves to be. Let us promise these things now, and keep the promises unbroken to the end."

Her solemn air touched Sir John. Too honorable and upright himself to suspect falsehood in others, he saw only the natural impulse of a lovely girl in Jean's words, and, taking the hand she gave him in both of his, he promised all she asked, and kept that promise to the end. She paused an instant, with a pale, absent expression, as if she searched herself, then looked up clearly in the confiding face above her, and promised what she faithfully performed in afteryears.

"When shall it be, little sweetheart? I leave all to you, only let it be soon, else some gay young lover will appear, and take you from me," said Sir John, playfully, anxious to chase away the dark expression which had stolen over Jean's face.

"Can you keep a secret?" asked the girl, smiling up at him, all her charming self again.

"Try me."

"I will. Edward is coming home in three days. I must be gone before he comes. Tell no one of this; he wishes to surprise them. And if you love me, tell nobody of your approaching marriage. Do not betray that you care for me until I am really yours. There will be such a stir, such remonstrances, explanations, and reproaches that I shall be worn out, and run away from you all to escape the trial. If I could have my wish, I would go to some quiet place tomorrow and wait till you come for me. I know so little of such things, I cannot tell how soon we may be married; not for some weeks, I think."

"Tomorrow, if we like. A special license permits people to marry when and where they please. My plan is better than yours. Listen, and tell me if it can be carried out. I will go to town tomorrow, get the license, invite my friend, the Reverend Paul Fairfax, to return with me, and tomorrow evening you come at your usual time, and, in the presence of my discreet old servants, make me the happiest man in England. How does this suit you, my little Lady Coventry?"

The plan which seemed made to meet her ends, the name which was the height of her ambition, and the blessed sense of safety which came to her filled Jean Muir with such intense satisfaction that tears of real feeling stood in her eyes, and the glad assent she gave was the truest word that had passed her lips for months.

"We will go abroad or to Scotland for our honeymoon, till the storm blows over," said Sir John, well knowing that this hasty marriage would surprise or offend all his relations, and feeling as glad as Jean to escape the first excitement.

"To Scotland, please. I long to see my father's home," said Jean, who dreaded to meet Sydney on the continent.

They talked a little longer, arranging all things, Sir John so intent on hurrying the event that Jean had nothing to do but give a ready assent to all his suggestions. One fear alone disturbed her. If Sir John went to town, he might meet Edward, might hear and believe his statements. Then all would be lost. Yet this risk must be incurred, if the marriage was to be speedily and safely accomplished; and to guard against the meeting was Jean's sole care. As they went through the park—for Sir John insisted upon taking her home—she said, clinging to his arm:

"Dear friend, bear one thing in mind, else we shall be much annoyed, and all our plans disarranged. Avoid your nephews; you are so frank your face will betray you. They both love me, are both hot-tempered, and in the first excitement of the discovery might be violent. You must incur no danger, no disrespect for my sake; so shun them both till we are safe—particularly Edward. He will feel that his brother has wronged him, and that you have succeeded where he failed. This will irritate him, and I fear a stormy scene. Promise to avoid both for a day or two; do not listen to them, do not see them, do not write to or receive letters from them. It is foolish, I know; but you are all I have, and I am haunted by a strange foreboding that I am to lose you."

Touched and flattered by her tender solicitude, Sir John promised everything, even while he laughed at her fears. Love blinded the good gentleman to the peculiarity of the request; the novelty, romance, and secrecy of the affair rather bewildered though it charmed him; and the knowledge that he had outrivaled three young and ardent lovers gratified his vanity more than he would confess. Parting from the girl at the garden gate, he turned homeward, feeling like a boy again, and loitered back, humming a love lay, quite forgetful of evening damps, gout, and the five-and-fifty years which lay so lightly on his shoulders since Jean's arms had rested there. She hurried toward the house, anxious to escape Coventry; but he was waiting for her, and she was forced to meet him.

"How could you linger so long, and keep me in suspense?" he said reproachfully, as he took her hand and tried to catch a glimpse of her face in the shadow of her hat brim. "Come and rest in the grotto. I have so much to say, to hear and enjoy."

"Not now; I am too tired. Let me go in and sleep. Tomorrow we will talk. It is damp and chilly, and my head aches with all this worry." Jean spoke wearily, yet with a touch of petulance, and Coventry, fancying that she was piqued at his not coming for her, hastened to explain with eager tenderness.

"My poor little Jean, you do need rest. We wear you out, among us, and you never complain. I should have come to bring you home, but Lucia detained me, and when I got away I saw my uncle had forestalled me. I shall be jealous of the old gentleman, if he is so devoted. Jean, tell me one thing before we part; I am free as air, now, and have a right to speak. Do you love me? Am I the happy man who has won your heart? I dare to think so, to believe that this telltale face of yours has betrayed you, and to hope that I have gained what poor Ned and wild Sydney have lost."

"Before I answer, tell me of your interview with Lucia. I have a right to know," said Jean.

Coventry hesitated, for pity and remorse were busy at his heart when he recalled poor Lucia's grief. Jean was bent on hearing the humiliation of her rival. As the young man paused, she frowned, then lifted up her face wreathed in softest smiles, and laying her hand on his arm, she said, with most effective emphasis, half shy, half fond, upon his name, "Please tell me, Gerald!"

He could not resist the look, the touch, the tone, and taking the little hand in his, he said rapidly, as if the task was distasteful to him, "I told her that I did not, could not love her; that I had submitted to my mother's wish, and, for a time, had felt tacitly bound to her, though no words had passed between us. But now I demanded my liberty, regretting that the separation was not mutually desired."

"And she—what did she say? How did she bear it?" asked Jean, feeling in her own woman's heart how deeply Lucia's must have been wounded by that avowal.

"Poor girl! It was hard to bear, but her pride sustained her to the end. She owned that no pledge tied me, fully relinquished any claim my past behavior had seemed to have given her, and prayed that I might find another woman to love me as truly, tenderly as she had done. Jean, I felt like a villain; and yet I never plighted my word to her, never really loved her, and had a perfect right to leave her, if I would."

"Did she speak of me?"

"Yes."

"What did she say?"

"Must I tell you?"

"Yes, tell me everything. I know she hates me and I forgive her, knowing that I should hate any woman whom *you* loved."

"Are you jealous, dear?"

"Of you, Gerald?" And the fine eyes glanced up at him, full of a brilliancy that looked like the light of love.

"You make a slave of me already. How do you do it? I never obeyed a woman before. Jean, I think you are a witch. Scotland is the home of weird, uncanny creatures, who take lovely shapes for the bedevilment of poor weak souls. Are you one of those fair deceivers?"

"You are complimentary," laughed the girl. "I *am* a witch, and one day my disguise will drop away and you will see me as I am, old, ugly, bad and lost. Beware of me in time. I've warned you. Now love me at your peril."

Coventry had paused as he spoke, and eyed her with an unquiet look, conscious of some fascination which conquered yet brought no happiness. A feverish yet pleasurable excitement possessed him; a reckless mood, making him eager to obliterate the past by any rash act, any new experience which his passion brought. Jean regarded him with a wistful, almost woeful face, for one short moment; then a strange smile broke over it, as she spoke in a tone of malicious mockery, under which lurked the bitterness of a sad truth. Coventry looked half bewildered, and his eye went from the girl's mysterious face to a dimly lighted window, behind whose curtains poor Lucia hid her aching heart, praying for him the tender prayers that loving women give to those whose sins are all forgiven for love's sake. His heart smote him, and a momentary feeling of repulsion came over him, as he looked at Jean. She saw it, felt angry, yet conscious of a sense of relief; for now that her own safety was so nearly secured, she felt no wish to do mischief, but rather a desire to undo what was already done, and be at peace with all the world. To recall him to his allegiance, she sighed and walked on, saying gently yet coldly, "Will you tell me what I ask before I answer your question, Mr. Coventry?"

"What Lucia said of you? Well, it was this. 'Beware of Miss Muir. We instinctively distrusted her when we had no cause. I believe in instincts, and mine have never changed, for she has not tried to delude me. Her art is wonderful; I feel yet cannot explain or detect it, except in the working of events which her hand seems to guide. She has brought sorrow and dissension into this hitherto happy family. We are all changed, and this girl has done it. Me she can harm no further; you she will ruin, if she can. Beware of her in time, or you win bitterly repent your blind infatuation!'"

"And what answer did you make?" asked Jean, as the last words came reluctantly from Coventry's lips.

"I told her that I loved you in spite of myself, and would make you my wife in the face of all opposition. Now, Jean, your answer."

"Give me three days to think of it. Good night." And gliding from him, she vanished into the house, leaving him to roam about half the night, tormented with remorse, suspense, and the old distrust which would return when Jean was not there to banish it by her art.

CHAPTER VIII

SUSPENSE

All the next day, Jean was in a state of the most intense anxiety, as every hour brought the crisis nearer, and every hour might bring defeat, for the subtlest human skill is often thwarted by some unforeseen accident. She longed to assure herself that Sir John was gone, but no servants came or went that day, and she could devise no pretext for sending to glean intelligence. She dared not go herself, lest the unusual act should excite suspicion, for she never went till evening. Even had she determined to venture, there was no time, for Mrs. Coventry was in one of her nervous states, and no one but Miss Muir could amuse her; Lucia was ill, and Miss Muir must give orders; Bella had a studious fit, and Jean must help her. Coventry lingered about the house for several hours, but Jean dared not send him, lest some hint of the truth might reach him. He had ridden away to his new duties when Jean did not appear, and the day dragged on wearisomely. Night came at last, and as Jean dressed for the late dinner, she hardly knew herself when she stood before her mirror, excitement lent such color and brilliancy to her countenance. Remembering the wedding which was to take place that evening, she put on a simple white dress and added a cluster of white roses in bosom and hair. She often wore flowers, but in spite of her desire to look and seem as usual, Bella's first words as she entered the drawing room were "Why, Jean, how like a bride you look; a veil and gloves would make you quite complete!"

"You forget one other trifle, Bell," said Gerald, with eyes that brightened as they rested on Miss Muir.

"What is that?" asked his sister.

"A bridegroom."

Bella looked to see how Jean received this, but she seemed quite composed as she smiled one of her sudden smiles, and merely said, "That trifle will doubtless be found when the time comes. Is Miss Beaufort too ill for dinner?"

"She begs to be excused, and said you would be willing to take her place, she thought."

As innocent Bella delivered this message, Jean glanced at Coventry, who evaded her eye and looked ill at ease.

A little remorse will do him good, and prepare him for repentance after the grand *coup*, she said to herself, and was particularly gay at dinnertime, though

Coventry looked often at Lucia's empty seat, as if he missed her. As soon as they left the table, Miss Muir sent Bella to her mother; and, knowing that Coventry would not linger long at his wine, she hurried away to the Hall. A servant was lounging at the door, and of him she asked, in a tone which was eager in spite of all efforts to be calm, "Is Sir John at home?"

"No, miss, he's just gone to town."

"Just gone! When do you mean?" cried Jean, forgetting the relief she felt in hearing of his absence in surprise at his late departure.

"He went half an hour ago, in the last train, miss."

"I thought he was going early this morning; he told me he should be back this evening."

"I believe he did mean to go, but was delayed by company. The steward came up on business, and a load of gentlemen called, so Sir John could not get off till night, when he wasn't fit to go, being worn out, and far from well."

"Do you think he will be ill? Did he look so?" And as Jean spoke, a thrill of fear passed over her, lest death should rob her of her prize.

"Well, you know, miss, hurry of any kind is bad for elderly gentlemen inclined to apoplexy. Sir John was in a worry all day, and not like himself. I wanted him to take his man, but he wouldn't; and drove off looking flushed and excited like. I'm anxious about him, for I know something is amiss to hurry him off in this way."

"When will he be back, Ralph?"

"Tomorrow noon, if possible; at night, certainly, he bid me tell anyone that called."

"Did he leave no note or message for Miss Coventry, or someone of the family?"

"No, miss, nothing."

"Thank you." And Jean walked back to spend a restless night and rise to meet renewed suspense.

The morning seemed endless, but noon came at last, and under the pretense of seeking coolness in the grotto, Jean stole away to a slope whence the gate to the Hall park was visible. For two long hours she watched, and no one came. She was just turning away when a horseman dashed through the gate and came galloping toward the Hall. Heedless of everything but the uncontrollable longing to gain some tidings, she ran to meet him, feeling assured that he brought ill news. It was a young man from the station, and as he caught sight of her, he drew bridle, looking agitated and undecided.

"Has anything happened?" she cried breathlessly.

"A dreadful accident on the railroad, just the other side of Croydon. News telegraphed half an hour ago," answered the man, wiping his hot face.

"The noon train? Was Sir John in it? Quick, tell me all!"

"It was that train, miss, but whether Sir John was in it or not, we don't know; for the guard is killed, and everything is in such confusion that nothing can be certain. They are at work getting out the dead and wounded. We heard that Sir John was expected, and I came up to tell Mr. Coventry, thinking he would wish to go down. A train leaves in fifteen minutes; where shall I find him? I was told he was at the Hall."

"Ride on, ride on! And find him if he is there. I'll run home and look for him. Lose no time. Ride! Ride!" And turning, Jean sped back like a deer, while the man tore up the avenue to rouse the Hall.

Coventry was there, and went off at once, leaving both Hall and house in dismay. Fearing to betray the horrible anxiety that possessed her, Jean shut herself up in her room and suffered untold agonies as the day wore on and no news came. At dark a sudden cry rang through the house, and Jean rushed down to learn the cause. Bella was standing in the hall, holding a letter, while a group of excited servants hovered near her.

"What is it?" demanded Miss Muir, pale and steady, though her heart died within her as she recognized Gerald's handwriting. Bella gave her the note, and hushed her sobbing to hear again the heavy tidings that had come.

> *Dear Bella:*
>
> *Uncle is safe; he did not go in the noon train. But several persons are sure that Ned was there. No trace of him as yet, but many bodies are in the river, under the ruins of the bridge, and I am doing my best to find the poor lad, if he is there. I have sent to all his haunts in town, and as he has not been seen, I hope it is a false report and he is safe with his regiment. Keep this from my mother till we are sure. I write you, because Lucia is ill. Miss Muir will comfort and sustain you. Hope for the best, dear.*
>
> *Yours, G.C.*

Those who watched Miss Muir as she read these words wondered at the strange expressions which passed over her face, for the joy which appeared there as Sir John's safety was made known did not change to grief or horror at poor Edward's possible fate. The smile died on her lips, but her voice did not falter, and in her downcast eyes shone an inexplicable look of something like triumph. No wonder, for if this was true, the danger which menaced her was averted for a time, and the marriage might be consummated without such desperate haste. This sad and sudden event seemed to her the mysterious fulfilment of a secret wish; and though startled she was not daunted but inspirited, for fate seemed to favor her designs. She did comfort Bella, control the excited household, and keep the rumors from Mrs. Coventry all that dreadful night.

At dawn Gerald came home exhausted, and bringing no tiding of the missing man. He had telegraphed to the headquarters of the regiment and received a reply, stating that Edward had left for London the previous day, meaning to go home before returning. The fact of his having been at the London station was also established, but whether he left by the train or not was still uncertain. The ruins were still being searched, and the body might yet appear.

"Is Sir John coming at noon?" asked Jean, as the three sat together in the rosy hush of dawn, trying to hope against hope.

"No, he had been ill, I learned from young Gower, who is just from town, and so had not completed his business. I sent him word to wait till night, for the bridge won't be passable till then. Now I must try and rest an hour; I've worked all night and have no strength left. Call me the instant any messenger arrives."

With that Coventry went to his room, Bella followed to wait on him, and Jean roamed through house and grounds, unable to rest. The morning was far spent when the messenger arrived. Jean went to receive his tidings, with the wicked hope still lurking at her heart.

"Is he found?" she asked calmly, as the man hesitated to speak.

"Yes, ma'am."

"You are sure?"

"I am certain, ma'am, though some won't say till Mr. Coventry comes to look."

"Is he alive?" And Jean's white lips trembled as she put the question.

"Oh no, ma'am, that warn't possible, under all them stones and water. The poor young gentleman is so wet, and crushed, and torn, no one would know him, except for the uniform, and the white hand with the ring on it."

Jean sat down, very pale, and the man described the finding of the poor shattered body. As he finished, Coventry appeared, and with one look of mingled remorse, shame, and sorrow, the elder brother went away, to find and bring the younger home. Jean crept into the garden like a guilty thing, trying to hide the satisfaction which struggled with a woman's natural pity, for so sad an end for this brave young life.

"Why waste tears or feign sorrow when I must be glad?" she muttered, as she paced to and fro along the terrace. "The poor boy is out of pain, and I am out of danger."

She got no further, for, turning as she spoke, she stood face to face with Edward! Bearing no mark of peril on dress or person, but stalwart and strong as ever, he stood there looking at her, with contempt and compassion struggling in his face. As if turned to stone, she remained motionless, with dilated eyes, arrested breath, and paling cheek. He did not speak but watched her silently till she put out a trembling hand, as if to assure herself by touch that it was really he. Then he drew back, and as if the act convinced as fully as words, she said slowly, "They told me you were dead."

"And you were glad to believe it. No, it was my comrade, young Courtney, who unconsciously deceived you all, and lost his life, as I should have done, if I had not gone to Ascot after seeing him off yesterday."

"To Ascot?" echoed Jean, shrinking back, for Edward's eye was on her, and his voice was stern and cold.

"Yes; you know the place. I went there to make inquiries concerning you and was well satisfied. Why are you still here?"

"The three days are not over yet. I hold you to your promise. Before night I shall be gone; till then you will be silent, if you have honor enough to keep your word."

"I have." Edward took out his watch and, as he put it back, said with cool precision, "It is now two, the train leaves for London at half-past six; a carriage will wait for you at the side door. Allow me to advise you to go then, for the instant dinner is over I shall speak." And with a bow he went into the house, leaving Jean nearly suffocated with a throng of contending emotions.

For a few minutes she seemed paralyzed; but the native energy of the woman forbade utter despair, till the last hope was gone. Frail as that now was, she still clung to it tenaciously, resolving to win the game in defiance of everything. Springing up, she went to her room, packed her few valuables, dressed herself with care, and then sat down to wait. She heard a joyful stir below, saw Coventry come hurrying back, and from a garrulous maid learned that the body was that of young Courtney. The uniform being the same as Edward's and the ring, a gift from him, had caused the men to believe the disfigured corpse to be that of the younger Coventry. No one but the maid came near her; once Bella's voice called her, but some one checked the girl, and the call was not repeated. At five an envelope was brought her, directed in Edward's hand, and containing a check which more than paid a year's salary. No word accompanied the gift, yet the generosity of it touched her, for Jean Muir had the relics of a once honest nature, and despite her falsehood could still admire nobleness and respect virtue. A tear of genuine shame dropped on the paper, and real gratitude filled her heart, as she thought that even if all else failed, she was not thrust out penniless into the world, which had no pity for poverty.

As the clock struck six, she heard a carriage drive around and went down to meet it. A servant put on her trunk, gave the order, "To the station, James," and she drove away without meeting anyone, speaking to anyone, or apparently being seen by anyone. A sense of utter weariness came over her, and she longed to lie down and forget. But the last chance still remained, and till that failed, she would not give up. Dismissing the carriage, she seated herself to watch for the quarter-past-six train from London, for in that Sir John would come if he came at all that night. She was haunted by the fear that Edward had met and told him. The first glimpse of Sir John's frank face would betray the truth. If he knew all, there was no hope, and she would go her way alone. If he knew nothing, there was yet time for the marriage; and once his wife, she knew she was safe, because for the honor of his name he would screen and protect her.

Up rushed the train, out stepped Sir John, and Jean's heart died within her. Grave, and pale, and worn he looked, and leaned heavily on the arm of a portly gentleman in black. The Reverend Mr. Fairfax, why has he come, if the secret is out? thought Jean, slowly advancing to meet them and fearing to read her fate in Sir John's face. He saw her, dropped his friend's arm, and hurried forward with the ardor of a young man, exclaiming, as he seized her hand with a beaming face, a glad voice, "My little girl! Did you think I would never come?"

She could not answer, the reaction was too strong, but she clung to him, regardless of time or place, and felt that her last hope had not failed. Mr. Fairfax proved himself equal to the occasion. Asking no questions, he hurried Sir John and Jean into a carriage and stepped in after them with a bland apology. Jean was soon herself again, and, having told her fears at his delay, listened eagerly while he related the various mishaps which had detained him.

"Have you seen Edward?" was her first question.

"Not yet, but I know he has come, and have heard of his narrow escape. I should have been in that train, if I had not been delayed by the indisposition which I then cursed, but now bless. Are you ready, Jean? Do you repent your choice, my child?"

"No, no! I am ready, I am only too happy to become your wife, dear, generous Sir John," cried Jean, with a glad alacrity, which touched the old man to the heart, and charmed the Reverend Mr. Fairfax, who concealed the romance of a boy under his clerical suit.

They reached the Hall. Sir John gave orders to admit no one and after a hasty dinner sent for his old housekeeper and his steward, told them of his purpose, and desired them to witness his marriage. Obedience had been the law of their lives, and Master could do nothing wrong in their eyes, so they played their parts willingly, for Jean was a favorite at the Hall. Pale as her gown, but calm and steady, she stood beside Sir John, uttering her vows in a clear tone and taking upon herself the vows of a wife with more than a bride's usual docility. When the ring was fairly on, a smile broke over her face. When Sir John kissed and called her his "little wife," she shed a tear or two of sincere happiness; and when Mr. Fairfax addressed her as "my lady," she laughed her musical laugh, and glanced up at a picture of Gerald with eyes full of exultation. As the servants left the room, a message was brought from Mrs. Coventry, begging Sir John to come to her at once.

"You will not go and leave me so soon?" pleaded Jean, well knowing why he was sent for.

"My darling, I must." And in spite of its tenderness, Sir John's manner was too decided to be withstood.

"Then I shall go with you," cried Jean, resolving that no earthly power should part them.

CHAPTER IX

LADY COVENTRY

When the first excitement of Edward's return had subsided, and before they could question him as to the cause of this unexpected visit, he told them that after dinner their curiosity should be gratified, and meantime he begged them to leave Miss Muir alone, for she had received bad news and must not be disturbed. The family with difficulty restrained their tongues and waited impatiently. Gerald confessed his love for Jean and asked his brother's pardon for betraying his trust. He had expected an outbreak, but Edward only looked at him with pitying eyes, and said sadly, "You too! I have no reproaches to make, for I know what you will suffer when the truth is known."

"What do you mean?" demanded Coventry.

"You will soon know, my poor Gerald, and we will comfort one another."

Nothing more could be drawn from Edward till dinner was over, the servants gone, and all the family alone together. Then pale and grave, but very self-possessed, for trouble had made a man of him, he produced a packet of letters, and said, addressing himself to his brother, "Jean Muir has deceived us all. I know her story; let me tell it before I read her letters."

"Stop! I'll not listen to any false tales against her. The poor girl has enemies who belie her!" cried Gerald, starting up.

"For the honor of the family, you must listen, and learn what fools she has made of us. I can prove what I say, and convince you that she has the art of a devil. Sit still ten minutes, then go, if you will."

Edward spoke with authority, and his brother obeyed him with a foreboding heart.

"I met Sydney, and he begged me to beware of her. Nay, listen, Gerald! I know she has told her story, and that you believe it; but her own letters convict her. She tried to charm Sydney as she did us, and nearly succeeded in inducing him to marry her. Rash and wild as he is, he is still a gentleman, and when an incautious word of hers roused his suspicions, he refused to make her his wife. A stormy scene ensued, and, hoping to intimidate him, she feigned to stab herself as if in despair. She did wound herself, but failed to gain her point and insisted upon going to a hospital to die. Lady Sydney, good, simple soul, believed the girl's version of the story, thought her son was in the wrong, and when he was gone, tried to atone for his fault by finding Jean Muir another home. She thought Gerald was soon to marry Lucia, and that I was away, so sent her here as a safe and comfortable retreat."

"But, Ned, are you sure of all this? Is Sydney to be believed?" began Coventry, still incredulous.

"To convince you, I'll read Jean's letters before I say more. They were written to an accomplice and were purchased by Sydney. There was a compact between the two women, that each should keep the other informed of all adventures, plots and plans, and share whatever good fortune fell to the lot of either. Thus Jean wrote freely, as you shall judge. The letters concern us alone. The first was written a few days after she came.

"Dear Hortense:

"Another failure. Sydney was more wily than I thought. All was going well, when one day my old fault beset me, I took too much wine, and I carelessly owned that I had been an actress. He was shocked, and retreated. I got up a scene, and gave myself a safe little wound, to frighten him. The brute was not frightened, but coolly left me to my fate. I'd have died to spite him, if I dared, but as I didn't, I lived to torment him. As yet, I have had no chance, but I will not forget him. His mother is a poor, weak creature, whom I could use as I would, and through her I found an excellent place. A sick mother, silly daughter, and two eligible sons. One is engaged to a handsome iceberg, but that only renders him more interesting in my eyes, rivalry adds so much to the charm of one's conquests. Well, my dear, I went, got up in the meek style, intending to do the pathetic; but before I saw the family, I was so angry I could hardly control myself. Through the indolence of Monsieur the young master, no carriage was sent for me, and I intend he shall atone for that rudeness by-and-by. The younger son, the mother, and the girl received me patronizingly, and I understood the simple souls at once. Monsieur (as I shall call him, as names are unsafe) was unapproachable, and took no pains to conceal his dislike of governesses. The cousin was lovely, but detestable with her pride, her coldness, and her very visible adoration of Monsieur, who let her worship him, like an inanimate idol as he is. I hated them both, of course, and in return for their insolence shall torment her with jealousy, and teach him how to woo a woman by making his heart ache. They are an intensely proud family, but I can humble them all, I think, by captivating the sons, and when they have committed themselves, cast them off, and marry the old uncle, whose title takes my fancy."

"She never wrote that! It is impossible. A woman could not do it," cried Lucia indignantly, while Bella sat bewildered and Mrs. Coventry supported herself with salts and fan. Coventry went to his brother, examined the writing, and returned to his seat, saying, in a tone of suppressed wrath, "She did write it. I posted some of those letters myself. Go on, Ned."

"I made myself useful and agreeable to the amiable ones, and over-

heard the chat of the lovers. It did not suit me, so I fainted away to stop it, and excite interest in the provoking pair. I thought I had succeeded, but Monsieur suspected me and showed me that he did. I forgot my meek role and gave him a stage look. It had a good effect, and I shall try it again. The man is well worth winning, but I prefer the title, and as the uncle is a hale, handsome gentleman, I can't wait for him to die, though Monsieur is very charming, with his elegant languor, and his heart so fast asleep no woman has had power to wake it yet. I told my story, and they believed it, though I had the audacity to say I was but nineteen, to talk Scotch, and bashfully confess that Sydney wished to marry me. Monsieur knows S. and evidently suspects something. I must watch him and keep the truth from him, if possible. "I was very miserable that night when I got alone. Something in the atmosphere of this happy home made me wish I was anything but what I am. As I sat there trying to pluck up my spirits, I thought of the days when I was lovely and young, good and gay. My glass showed me an old woman of thirty, for my false locks were off, my paint gone, and my face was without its mask. Bah! how I hate sentiment! I drank your health from your own little flask, and went to bed to dream that I was playing Lady Tartuffe—as I am. Adieu, more soon."

No one spoke as Edward paused, and taking up another letter, he read on:

"My Dear Creature:

"All goes well. Next day I began my task, and having caught a hint of the character of each, tried my power over them. Early in the morning I ran over to see the Hall. Approved of it highly, and took the first step toward becoming its mistress, by piquing the curiosity and flattering the pride of its master. His estate is his idol; I praised it with a few artless compliments to himself, and he was charmed. The cadet of the family adores horses. I risked my neck to pet his beast, and he was charmed. The little girl is romantic about flowers; I made a posy and was sentimental, and she was charmed. The fair icicle loves her departed mamma, I had raptures over an old picture, and she thawed. Monsieur is used to being worshipped. I took no notice of him, and by the natural perversity of human nature, he began to take notice of me. He likes music; I sang, and stopped when he'd listened long enough to want more. He is lazily fond of being amused; I showed him my skill, but refused to exert it in his behalf. In short, I gave him no peace till he began to wake up. In order to get rid of the boy, I fascinated him, and he was sent away. Poor lad, I rather liked him, and if the title had been nearer would have married him.

"Many thanks for the honor." And Edward's lip curled with intense scorn. But Gerald sat like a statue, his teeth set, his eyes fiery, his brows bent, waiting for the end.

"The passionate boy nearly killed his brother, but I turned the affair to good account, and bewitched Monsieur by playing nurse, till Vash-

ti (the icicle) interfered. Then I enacted injured virtue, and kept out of his way, knowing that he would miss me, I mystified him about S. by sending a letter where S. would not get it, and got up all manner of soft scenes to win this proud creature. I get on well and meanwhile privately fascinate Sir J. by being daughterly and devoted. He is a worthy old man, simple as a child, honest as the day, and generous as a prince. I shall be a happy woman if I win him, and you shall share my good fortune; so wish me success.

"This is the third, and contains something which will surprise you," Edward said, as he lifted another paper.

"Hortense:

"I've done what I once planned to do on another occasion. You know my handsome, dissipated father married a lady of rank for his second wife. I never saw Lady H——d but once, for I was kept out of the way. Finding that this good Sir J. knew something of her when a girl, and being sure that he did not know of the death of her little daughter, I boldly said I was the child, and told a pitiful tale of my early life. It worked like a charm; he told Monsieur, and both felt the most chivalrous compassion for Lady Howard's daughter, though before they had secretly looked down on me, and my real poverty and my lowliness. That boy pitied me with an honest warmth and never waited to learn my birth. I don't forget that and shall repay it if I can. Wishing to bring Monsieur's affair to a successful crisis, I got up a theatrical evening and was in my element. One little event I must tell you, because I committed an actionable offense and was nearly discovered. I did not go down to supper, knowing that the moth would return to flutter about the candle, and preferring that the fluttering should be done in private, as Vashti's jealousy is getting uncontrollable. Passing throught the gentlemen's dressing room, my quick eye caught sight of a letter lying among the costumes. It was no stage affair, and an odd sensation of fear ran through me as I recognized the hand of S. I had feared this, but I believe in chance; and having found the letter, I examined it. You know I can imitate almost any hand. When I read in this paper the whole story of my affair with S., truly told, and also that he had made inquiries into my past life and discovered the truth, I was in a fury. To be so near success and fail was terrible, and I resolved to risk everything. I opened the letter by means of a heated knife blade under the seal, therefore the envelope was perfect; imitating S.'s hand, I penned a few lines in his hasty style, saying he was at Baden, so that if Monsieur answered, the reply would not reach him, for he is in London, it seems. This letter I put into the pocket whence the other must have fallen, and was just congratulating myself on this narrow escape, when Dean, the maid of Vashti, appeared as if watching me. She had evidently seen the letter in my hand, and suspected something. I took no notice of her, but must be careful, for she is on the watch. After this the evening closed with strictly private theatricals, in which Monsieur and myself were the

> *only actors. To make sure that he received my version of the story first,*
> *I told him a romantic story of S.'s persecution, and he believed it. This*
> *I followed up by a moonlight episode behind a rose hedge, and sent the*
> *young gentleman home in a half-dazed condition. What fools men are!"*

"She is right!" muttered Coventry, who had flushed scarlet with shame and anger, as his folly became known and Lucia listened in astonished silence.

"Only one more, and my distasteful task will be nearly over," said Edward, unfolding the last of the papers. "This is not a letter, but a copy of one written three nights ago. Dean boldly ransacked Jean Muir's desk while she was at the Hall, and, fearing to betray the deed by keeping the letter, she made a hasty copy which she gave me today, begging me to save the family from disgrace. This makes the chain complete. Go now, if you will, Gerald. I would gladly spare you the pain of hearing this."

"I will not spare myself; I deserve it. Read on," replied Coventry, guessing what was to follow and nerving himself to hear it. Reluctantly his brother read these lines:

> *"The enemy has surrendered! Give me joy, Hortense; I can be the*
> *wife of this proud monsieur, if I will. Think what an honor for the di-*
> *vorced wife of a disreputable actor. I laugh at the farce and enjoy it, for*
> *I only wait till the prize I desire is fairly mine, to turn and reject this*
> *lover who has proved himself false to brother, mistress, and his own con-*
> *science. I resolved to be revenged on both, and I have kept my word. For*
> *my sake he cast off the beautiful woman who truly loved him; he forgot*
> *his promise to his brother, and put by his pride to beg of me the worn-*
> *out heart that is not worth a good man's love. Ah well, I am satisfied, for*
> *Vashti has suffered the sharpest pain a proud woman can endure, and*
> *will feel another pang when I tell her that I scorn her recreant lover, and*
> *give him back to her, to deal with as she will."*

Coventry started from his seat with a fierce exclamation, but Lucia bowed her face upon her hands, weeping, as if the pang had been sharper than even Jean foresaw.

"Send for Sir John! I am mortally afraid of this creature. Take her away; do something to her. My poor Bella, what a companion for you! Send for Sir John at once!" cried Mrs. Coventry incoherently, and clasped her daughter in her arms, as if Jean Muir would burst in to annihilate the whole family. Edward alone was calm.

"I have already sent, and while we wait, let me finish this story. It is true that Jean is the daughter of Lady Howard's husband, the pretended clergyman, but really a worthless man who married her for her money. Her own child died, but this girl, having beauty, wit and a bold spirit, took her fate into her own hands, and became an actress. She married an actor, led a reckless life for some years; quarreled with her husband, was divorced, and went to Paris; left the stage, and tried to support herself as governess and companion. You know how she fared with the

Sydneys, how she has duped us, and but for this discovery would have duped Sir John. I was in time to prevent this, thank heaven. She is gone; no one knows the truth but Sydney and ourselves; he will be silent, for his own sake; we will be for ours, and leave this dangerous woman to the fate which will surely overtake her."

"Thank you, it has overtaken her, and a very happy one she finds it."

A soft voice uttered the words, and an apparition appeared at the door, which made all start and recoil with amazement—Jean Muir leaning on the arm of Sir John.

"How dare you return?" began Edward, losing the self-control so long preserved. "How dare you insult us by coming back to enjoy the mischief you have done? Uncle, you do not know that woman!"

"Hush, boy, I will not listen to a word, unless you remember where you are," said Sir John with a commanding gesture.

"Remember your promise: love me, forgive me, protect me, and do not listen to their accusations," whispered Jean, whose quick eye had discovered the letters.

"I will; have no fears, my child," he answered, drawing her nearer as he took his accustomed place before the fire, always lighted when Mrs. Coventry was down.

Gerald, who had been pacing the room excitedly, paused behind Lucia's chair as if to shield her from insult; Bella clung to her mother; and Edward, calming himself by a strong effort, handed his uncle the letters, saying briefly, "Look at those, sir, and let them speak."

"I will look at nothing, hear nothing, believe nothing which can in any way lessen my respect and affection for this young lady. She has prepared me for this. I know the enemy who is unmanly enough to belie and threaten her. I know that you both are unsuccessful lovers, and this explains your unjust, uncourteous treatment now. We all have committed faults and follies. I freely forgive Jean hers, and desire to know nothing of them from your lips. If she has innocently offended, pardon it for my sake, and forget the past."

"But, Uncle, we have proofs that this woman is not what she seems. Her own letters convict her. Read them, and do not blindly deceive yourself," cried Edward, indignant at his uncle's words.

A low laugh startled them all, and in an instant they saw the cause of it. While Sir John spoke, Jean had taken the letters from the hand which he had put behind him, a favorite gesture of his, and, unobserved, had dropped them on the fire. The mocking laugh, the sudden blaze, showed what had been done. Both young men sprang forward, but it was too late; the proofs were ashes, and Jean Muir's bold, bright eyes defied them, as she said, with a disdainful little gesture. "Hands off, gentlemen! You may degrade yourselves to the work of detectives, but I am not a prisoner yet. Poor Jean Muir you might harm, but Lady Coventry is beyond your reach."

"Lady Coventry!" echoed the dismayed family, in varying tones of incredulity, indignation, and amazement.

"Aye, my dear and honored wife," said Sir John, with a protecting arm about the slender figure at his side; and in the act, the words, there was a tender dignity that touched the listeners with pity and respect for the deceived man. "Receive her as such, and for my sake, forbear all further accusation," he continued steadily. "I know what I have done. I have no fear that I shall repent it. If I am blind, let me remain so till time opens my eyes. We are going away for a little while, and when we return, let the old life return again, unchanged, except that Jean makes sunshine for me as well as for you."

No one spoke, for no one knew what to say. Jean broke the silence, saying coolly, "May I ask how those letters came into your possession?"

"In tracing out your past life, Sydney found your friend Hortense. She was poor, money bribed her, and your letters were given up to him as soon as received. Traitors are always betrayed in the end," replied Edward sternly.

Jean shrugged her shoulders, and shot a glance at Gerald, saying with her significant smile, "Remember that, monsieur, and allow me to hope that in wedding you will be happier than in wooing. Receive my congratulations, Miss Beaufort, and let me beg of you to follow my example, if you would keep your lovers."

Here all the sarcasm passed from her voice, the defiance from her eye, and the one unspoiled attribute which still lingered in this woman's artful nature shone in her face, as she turned toward Edward and Bella at their mother's side.

"You have been kind to me," she said, with grateful warmth. "I thank you for it, and will repay it if I can. To you I will acknowledge that I am not worthy to be this good man's wife, and to you I will solemnly promise to devote my life to his happiness. For his sake forgive me, and let there be peace between us."

There was no reply, but Edward's indignant eyes fell before hers. Bella half put out her hand, and Mrs. Coventry sobbed as if some regret mingled with her resentment. Jean seemed to expect no friendly demonstration, and to understand that they forbore for Sir John's sake, not for hers, and to accept their contempt as her just punishment.

"Come home, love, and forget all this," said her husband, ringing the bell, and eager to be gone. "Lady Coventry's carriage."

And as he gave the order, a smile broke over her face, for the sound assured her that the game was won. Pausing an instant on the threshold before she vanished from their sight, she looked backward, and fixing on Gerald the strange glance he remembered well, she said in her penetrating voice, "Is not the last scene better than the first?"

Lector House believes that a society develops through a two-fold approach of continuous learning and adaptation, which is derived from the study of classic literary works spread across the historic timeline of literature records. Therefore, we aim at reviving, repairing and redeveloping all those inaccessible or damaged but historically as well as culturally important literature across subjects so that the future generations may have an opportunity to study and learn from past works to embark upon a journey of creating a better future.

This book is a result of an effort made by Lector House towards making a contribution to the preservation and repair of original ancient works which might hold historical significance to the approach of continuous learning across subjects.

HAPPY READING & LEARNING!

LECTOR HOUSE LLP
E-MAIL: lectorpublishing@gmail.com